"Are you Falconer?" she challenged rudely

"None other," he replied coolly, his eyes appraising her slender frame as he slowly rose from behind his desk.

"You louse," she shot at him. "You unmitigated louse!" Though his eyes narrowed at the way she was insulting him, she rushed on, "And you call yourself a gentleman...."

"That's enough," he ordered.

Kelsey ignored his command. "I haven't even started on the substitute names I have for—"

That was as far as she got. To feel that admittedly attractive mouth over hers, to feel strong muscled arms around her—arms there was no breaking away from— was totally unexpected. And not totally unpleasant....

Books by Jessica Steele

HARLEQUIN PRESENTS

HARLEQUIN ROMANCES

These books may be available at your local bookseller.

For a free catalog listing all titles currently available,
send your name and address to:

Harlequin Reader Service
P.O. Box 52040, Phoenix, AZ   85072-2040
Canadian address: P.O. Box 2800, Postal Station A,
5170 Yonge St., Willowdale, Ont.   M2N 5T5

JESSICA STEELE

imprudent challenge

Harlequin Books

TORONTO • NEW YORK • LONDON
AMSTERDAM • PARIS • SYDNEY • HAMBURG
STOCKHOLM • ATHENS • TOKYO • MILAN

Harlequin Presents first edition July 1984
ISBN 0-373-10709-9

Original hardcover edition published in 1984
by Mills & Boon Limited

CHAPTER ONE

JAPAN, Kelsey had heard, was beautiful. But on that Sunday in June, on the last leg of her journey, a journey which had left her feeling she had been travelling non-stop for a week—when in reality she had only left England two days ago, she had seen barely anything of Japan at all.

Vaguely she recalled the forests of trees that had covered either side of the motorway on the first part of the hour-long bus ride from Narita airport to the air terminal in Tokyo City, but her mind had been too consumed with her quest, the real reason why she was here, for her to appreciate scenery.

Needing to catch up on some sleep if she was to arrive in Komatsu alert and not like some zombie, she had chosen not to fly on to her final destination but to spend the previous night in a hotel in Tokyo and to continue by bullet train this morning. Remembering the hotel, Kelsey had her mind briefly taken away from her worries about her parents and their apparent marriage break-up—which she just could not, and would not, believe in—by the sight of the freshly laundered, neatly folded *yukata* that lay on her bed at the hotel. It was a garment, so her mother had told her, in one of the rare moments over the last three months when she had got her to tell her anything of Japan, in which one not only slept in, but used also as a type of housecoat, no one minding in the least if one cared to take a walk around the block in such a garment.

Yet another purveyor of food and drink walked down the aisle of the train compartment Kelsey was in. She had lost count of how many people, all selling different kinds of comestibles, had passed through the carriage. She lost interest too, as the train sped on to Komatsu, and she wondered if perhaps she should have let her father know that she was coming.

There had been a telephone on the train from Tokyo to Nagoya, and very probably there was a phone on this train too. But somehow she had a feeling that she might be able to find out more of what was going on between her parents if her arrival took her father by surprise.

Not that either of them owed her an explanation. Independent-minded herself, she had always been of the opinion that everyone was their own person. But her parents had never seemed like separate people, somehow. So much in love, they had seemed as one. She recalled their one and only visit home some four years ago when at sixteen she had been studying for her 'A' levels; perhaps she had been more aware then than two years previously when they had left England, but she had seen then, and had been delighted in, the love they had for each other.

She had been a romantic at sixteen, admittedly. Very likely she still was. Maybe that was why, although never short of boy-friends, she had been unable to make that same sort of commitment some of her friends made. She had wanted a love like the love her parents had, but so far it hadn't happened. Idealistic perhaps, but, having seen the way her mother had to only walk into the room and without saying a word, her father's eyes would say 'I love you,' she wouldn't settle for anything less. There had to be a love like that for her out there somewhere.

Kelsey's soft brown eyes went dreamy as she thought of that time four years ago when her parents had come home for a holiday, and to see her and Gran. And she went on to recollect how, because of her 'O' levels and their concern not to disturb her schooling, they had left her with Gran when her father had changed jobs and gone out to Japan when she was fourteen. She had watched them go with mixed feelings; aware even then that really they had not needed a third to complete their happiness, though for all that, they had never let her feel she was being left out. She knew herself loved too—her mother's moist eyes, her father's arms round the two of them as they had said goodbye, were proof enough of that.

She had been going to follow them out when her 'O' levels were over, but that had never materialised, because then there were 'A' levels, and by then she had settled down happily with Gran. And so instead of going back with them four years ago, she had stayed behind to study, and to remember, whenever she thought of her parents, the little things. Small things, like the way one would wait for the other to complete what they were saying, even if their opinions differed, which they rarely did. Little things like the time her father had bumped his forehead on a cupboard, and swore, and her eyes had gone wide because she knew the word but didn't at sixteen for some reason think that he did, and the way her mother had said, 'Shall I tell you off for swearing in front of the baby, or,' archly Kelsey realised later, 'shall I kiss it better?' She remembered oh, so clearly the way her mother had giggled, giggled like a schoolgirl herself, and she would have been forty-four then, as her father had wiggled his eyebrows comically and said, 'It really does hurt,' although there hadn't been so much as a red mark on his forehead. They had gone off together, their arms draped around each other, and Kelsey had gone to help Gran in the kitchen.

The dreamy look left Kelsey's eyes as she remembered her mother as she had left her in England two days before. And accepting that since Gran had died three months ago, loving her as they all did, sorrow had left its mark on them, Kelsey knew it was more than that that made her mother permanently depressed.

She wondered, as she had many times, had she been

right to telephone her mother when the doctor had said there wasn't much hope that Gran was going to make it through her illness. Perhaps if her mother hadn't rushed home, starting her journey the very next day, the problems between her parents would have sorted themselves out.

Reason told her she could have done nothing else, since with Gran calling for 'Eve' as she lay dying, she had died in peace with her daughter Eve there at the last, holding her hand.

But that didn't stop the twinge of guilt that she had been the cause of separating her parents for the first time in their married life. Though in truth, she had thought her father might come home too if he could manage the time off.

Kelsey recalled how, when the shock of Gran's death had receded, although it was expected, not liking her secretarial job she had started to grow hopeful that when her mother returned to Japan, she might ask her to go with her. But when two months had passed and no mention made about her mother going back, perturbed as Kelsey was starting to grow that the telephone wires between England and Japan were not red-hot as she would have supposed, and no letter posted to Japan save the one she herself had written telling her father of Gran's death, that, plus the fact that her mother never mentioned her father's name, she had just had to say something. Her mother's reply to her question about return flights had left her totally floored and, for several seconds, totally speechless.

'I'm—not going back' Eve Marchant had said, when for a moment it had looked as though she was going to be evasive.

Shattered, Kelsey had stared at the trim, still beautiful woman facing her, her world going upside down for crazy seconds as she fought to avoid the implication behind her mother's remark. As far as she knew, her father was contracted to stay in Japan for some years yet.

'Not—going back?' she exclaimed in disbelief when her mother had nothing to add. 'But—what about Dad?'

Eve Marchant had shrugged, for all the world as though she didn't care tuppence for her husband, when Kelsey knew full well that she did—she had to; theirs was a perfect match. It was, it had to be—for years they had been an ideal couple in her mind.

'He knows,' her mother replied after a long silence.

'You've told him? You told him before you left that you weren't going back?' Kelsey probed, winded, the first pangs of guilt assaulting her that it was she who had separated them.

'Not in so many words. But he knows.'

Kelsey sifted through her mother's reply. Her parents always had been telepathic with each other's thoughts, that was all part of what made them one. Yes, she thought, he would know without her mother having to tell him. But if they were still telepathic with each other, then surely that must mean that there was still something there? That they still loved each other!

'But why? I mean . . .' Kelsey was floundering, 'I mean, you've always been so happy together. Why, you and Dad are . . .'

'Are separated—permanently,' Eve Marchant interrupted. And before Kelsey, her mouth already starting to shape the protesting 'No', could butt in, she went on quickly, doing little for Kelsey's feeling of guilt that she had been instrumental in causing the break, 'I've been wanting to come home for ages—and he knew it.'

Henry, Kelsey wanted to say when her mother referred to her father as 'he', my father's name is Henry. 'But—but couldn't you have come home together? Dad must have some leave due, and if he hasn't, in the compassionate circumstances of Gran dy . . .'

'I wanted to come home permanently—not for just a holiday.'

'But you love Japan! You've said often what a beautiful country it is!' Kelsey could clearly recall letters, beautiful descriptive letters that helped her to share in the rapture of scenic wonders her mother had written of.

'Yes—I do,' she heard her confess. 'But—well, things haven't been going right with your father and me for some time, and . . .'

'You never said anything in your letters . . .'

'I'm supposed to give you an account of everything that takes place between your father and me, am I?' Eve Marchant replied, staggering Kelsey afresh to hear an unheard-of before waspish note in her voice.

Momentarily she wondered if Gran's dying had rocked her mother's foundations, for Gran had always been there. And then her mother's tone was softening.

'We've—I've,' she quickly corrected, 'hardly seen anything of you. We . . .' she bit her lip, 'I missed your adolescence altogether.'

Kelsey's eyes widened at this new idea that her mother wanting to see more of her was the reason for her parents' break-up. It was the first she had heard that her mother pined for the sight of her.

'You told Dad you wanted to come back permanently because of me!'

Eve Marchant looked away from her surprised look. 'We discussed you—many times,' she replied. 'Is it so unnatural that I should want to know something of you?'

Kelsey's surprise faded as her mother turned her head to look at her. There was a look of love for her there in her mother's eyes, and she knew herself loved, even while knowing that that could not be the prime reason for her wanting to return to England.

'Besides which,' Eve Marchant added with a wry smile that said her sense of humour wasn't completely buried, 'the climate out there was playing havoc with my skin!'

That she did look a little older this time than she had four years previously was no more than a normal ageing process, Kelsey thought. But her mother was still beautiful. Though, never thinking of her as being a vain woman, she paused then to wonder, being beautiful all her life, was she now starting to fret that her looks might be fading? Was that what was at the root of it all? She had said that things hadn't been going right for them for some time, but ... Suddenly Kelsey was remembering a conversation Gran had started, when gossip was rife about a woman down the street—a woman about the same age as Eve—who had 'gone off' with a man twenty years younger. Gran had sniffed as she'd set the seal to the conversation by saying, 'She's at that funny age.'

Was her mother at 'that funny age'? Sudden alarm made her ask the question, 'There isn't anyone else, is there?' And at the blank expression her mother wore, 'I mean—there isn't some other man ...'

The indignant look she received was all the answer she could wish for. It underlined for her what she already knew, that her mother would never love anyone but Henry Marchant.

'Then why ...?'

'Your father thinks more of his job than he does of me—he's proved it.'

'Because he wouldn't agree to return permanently? But he's under contract, isn't he?'

'Contracts have been broken before.' Kelsey could hear the waspish note returning. It was there stronger when, a touch bitterly, her mother added, getting in first before Kelsey could voice her next question; 'And don't think he can't afford it, because while I admit he's sending me a hefty allowance through the bank here each month, he has a tidy amount saved for when his contract officially ends.'

With her mother starting to get bitter and twisted, proof that her husband no longer loved her lying in the fact that when he could well afford it, he would not give up his job and return to England, therefore it was clear that he was putting his job before her; Kelsey, loving her every bit as much as she loved her father, could not bear to see her getting so uptight, and she left the conversation there.

But, in the week that followed, although the subject was not referred to again, that did not stop her from constantly thinking about her parents' marriage. How could their marriage be over? Why, they had always been like two young lovebirds! It pained her greatly that the pedestal she had set her parents' marriage on—guidelines for her own marriage if and when it happened—appeared to have crumpled, the love they had fractured amid the ruins.

It was at the end of that week, coming home from work and finding her mother looking as though she had spent most of the day in tears, that Kelsey knew that she was going to have to do something about it. Though at that moment she had no idea what.

But on the Monday of the next week, when she still had no clear idea in her head what she could do but give her mother all the moral support she could, her boss, an underhand man she had no liking for, came bombasting into her small office and tried tearing her off a strip for something that wasn't her fault, and she found she had retaliated angrily and had given in her notice.

And having given in her notice, Kelsey found that when her temper had cooled down, she did not regret her action one little bit. And from there, making her wonder why she hadn't thought of it before, as if the idea had been in her head all the time just waiting for the fog of having her parents solely on her mind to clear, she knew what she was going to do.

The way things were, thousands of miles separating

them, her father staying put and her mother refusing to budge, their only communication—for no mail had come from Japan—through the bank in the shape of the money transferred to England every month, they were never going to get back together.

By the time Kelsey arrived home that evening she was uncaring whether she was being romantically idealistic or not in her refusal to accept, when marriages were breaking up all around her, that her parents' marriage was over. Though it called for a great deal of tact when she explained how, having thrown up her job, having previously mentioned how unbearable she had found her boss, she thought she might take a holiday before she looked for something new. The sticky part came when, in agreement with everything she had said so far, her mother heard just what location for her holiday she had in mind.

'You're going to *Japan!*'

'I thought I'd go and see Dad,' said Kelsey, swallowing down the 'How about coming with me?' that hovered when her mother's mouth took on a tight look. 'If, as you say,' she went on, 'Dad is staying to finish out his contract, it will be years before I see him again.' With her mother starting to look hurt and even more tight-lipped it was an effort for Kelsey to make herself go on. But having got this far, she made herself continue, 'With Gran insisting on putting some money in my name when I was eighteen, I should have enough to cover my expenses. And with Gran leaving the house to you, and Dad making you an allowance each month, you should be all right while I'm away.'

That waspish note was back in Eve Marchant's voice as she snapped, 'You don't have to worry about me,' and, sounding peevish, 'Nobody has to worry about me.'

Though she wanted to put her arms around her, the years they had been apart had Kelsey stifling the impulse. Though not the words, 'I can't help it—I love you.'

For a moment she thought her mother was going to crack. But she didn't. 'I'm glad somebody does,' she replied. But though that waspish note was still there, Kelsey knew it wasn't the love of a daughter she wanted, it was the love of her husband.

She caught herself sighing again as she had then, just as an announcement came over the loudspeaker. The announcement was in Japanese, but having learnt when leaving the bullet train in Nagoya to transfer to this one that if you didn't look sharp you stood a good chance of not getting off at all—she could swear the train was in and out of the station in one minute flat—Kelsey began to collect her things together, suspecting that the next stop would be Komatsu.

It was. And having exited from the ticket barrier, Kelsey was relieved to see that the taxi rank her mother had informed her about was right outside. Putting down her cases, she handed the taxi driver her father's card, his name and address printed in Japanese, which her mother had given her—further proof, since she still had it, that she loved him.

Kelsey sat back in the cab, her excitement growing at the thought of seeing her father. She had the same fair hair as her mother, though nature had thought to streak hers with natural blonde highlights and wave at the front, so that the style she now wore left her hair just turning under below her shoulders and waving down the sides of her face. She rather thought she had started wearing her hair in a topknot when she had waved her father goodbye, with some idea in her head, after hearing her mother call her 'the baby', of looking more grown-up with her hair that way.

The taxi stopped outside a substantially built two-storied house in an area on the outskirts of Komatsu, and the snapshots she had at home came to life, the large persimmon tree in the garden green and luxurious in the rain. Nobody had told her about the rain.

She leaned over to open the taxi door, forgetting that in Tokyo she had received the same feeling of surprise when the white-gloved driver had used a switch which had the doors opening automatically.

Having parted with some of her yen, she stood looking at the house for a moment, wondering if her father was in. There was a small Honda car on the drive, so she rather guessed that he was.

Excitement surged up in her as she picked up her cases and went forward. Excitement, and love, and— hope. Hope that if he still loved her mother, as she was sure he must, then she could do something to get them back together again.

Setting down her cases again, she rang the bell, her ears straining for sounds of movement in the silence that followed; soon she heard light pattering footsteps, and then the door was being opened. But it was not her father who stood there.

'Kon-nichiwa,' said the exquisite Japanese girl of about her own twenty years. And as the word hit Kelsey and had her searching her crash course of elementary Japanese phrases and coming up with the translation 'Good afternoon' the girl was doing a rapid retake—Westerners not being too common a sight in Komatsu, so Kelsey's mother had told her—and was smiling as she amended with a small bow, in near perfect English, 'Good afternoon,' and adding, 'May I help you?'

'I've come to see Mr Henry Marchant,' explained Kelsey, smiling in her relief that the girl could speak English. She didn't know yet who she was, but from the photographs she had, she knew she had come to the right house.

'Ah, Marchant-san.' replied the girl, and smiling still, 'I am afraid you have come to the wrong address. Marchant-san no longer lives here.'

'No longer ...!' Kelsey started to gasp. 'But my mother gave me his card with this address on!'

'Your mother?' the girl enquired politely.

'I'm Henry Marchant's daughter ...' was as far as she got before the smile on the Japanese girl's face became a positive beam of delight.

'I have heard much about you from your mother,' she said. 'But please to come in from the rain.'

It seemed a good idea, for although the rain had fined down to a drizzle, she stood a very good chance of getting soaked if she stayed outside much longer.

Following suit, Kelsey left her sandals in the lobby as the Japanese girl did, knowing from correspondence with her parents that it was unheard-of to walk in anything but socks or bare feet on the straw *tatami* matting to be found in most Japanese homes. Though the sitting room to which the girl, who introduced herself as Yukiko Akita, took her, was furnished in Western style. And in next to no time Kelsey found herself seated on a settee, a glass of cold wheat tea in her hand and two of the tiniest of cakes in front of her.

But as refreshing as she found the tea, she had too many questions burning to be answered to want to observe the pleasantries. For a start, where was her father? And why on earth, when this was the only home he had known since moving to Japan, had he suddenly decided to move?

'You know where my father lives, Miss Akita?' she asked, when the black-fringed dainty girl had seated herself opposite.

'Certainly,' she replied. 'But please call me Yukiko.' And with another smile, she added, 'Marchant-*san*'s home is not far from here. It will be my pleasure to drive you there.'

Awash with relief again that she did not have to hunt up the whole of the Ishikawa Prefecture, where Komatsu was situated, to find her father, Kelsey returned Yukiko's smile. And in turn, as she wondered—since it must look odd that she didn't know her father had moved—how to retrieve that situation, she invited her to call her Kelsey.

Then embarrassed, at the implied lie pride was forcing on her, falteringly she said, 'I must have given the taxi driver the card—with the wrong address on it.'

'An easy mistake when you have two cards,' smiled Yukiko. 'Marchant-*san* will regret now, I think, that he has moved into somewhere smaller, because this house was too large for him now that your mother is not here.'

'Because of my visit, you mean?' queried Kelsey slowly, slightly surprised that by the sound of it her father, a proud man, must have told one and all that his wife had left him.

'I am so sorry,' said Yukiko all of a sudden, her smile departing for the first time. 'I have not offered my condolences for your loss of your grandmother. It must have been a sad time for you and your mother.'

Kelsey murmured that it had been. Then Yukiko, still in sympathetic vein, was going on to reveal that Henry Marchant was every bit as proud as his daughter had thought, when she said:

'And so sad for Marchant-*san* too, that like most legal matters, it will take so long for his wife to clear up her mother's estate, and that she will have to stay in England while it is all settled.'

'These things—do take time,' said Kelsey, her mind taking in that her father had excused his wife's prolonged absence with the story that there were many long-drawn-out legal matters to be dealt with in connection with Gran's estate.

'But you are here now to cheer him.' Yukiko was smiling again, her words causing Kelsey to wonder if her father was looking as unhappy as her mother was.

Then the Japanese girl was glancing at her empty glass and was offering her some more *mugi cha*. But when Kelsey smilingly refused more tea, she said:

'You are anxious now to see your father, I think.'

Hoping she wasn't being impolite, just as she was hoping that her inner anxieties weren't showing, Kelsey murmured, 'If it's no trouble . . .'

Her cases stowed in the Honda, Kelsey was fast wishing she had not been so set on not letting her father know she was coming. He was ever a proud man, and it was clear he didn't want anyone to know that his wife was not coming back. Only by the skin of her teeth had she been able to keep that secret safe. Though to her mind, with her mother adamant about not returning, it was a secret that was bound to come out in time.

The car drew to a halt outside a small ridged-tiled bungalow, and Kelsey, determined that somehow some compromise should be found, helped Yukiko to remove her cases from the car.

'Forgive me if I do not stay to say hello to Marchant-*san*,' said Yukiko with her warm smile. And, a faint flush coming to her cheeks as though she was nursing some happy private thoughts, 'My own father is due home shortly, and—I wish to be there when he returns.'

Conscious of the look of excitement that accompanied the other girl's blush, Kelsey was conscious also that although the Japanese girl had made no attempt to rush her and had been more than courteous to a complete stranger, she had intruded far too much on her time. Though before she could apologise, Yukiko was bowing in farewell and asking, with nothing but friendliness, which did away with any thoughts Kelsey might have that her unexpected arrival had been a nuisance:

'Perhaps I may be permitted to call on you during your stay?'

Kelsey also wanted to be on her way. She too wanted to see her parent. But the friendliness of Yukiko found an answering friendliness in her as, sincerely, she replied, 'I should like that.'

It was more of a path than a drive to the front door of the small bungalow, and the Honda was still in first gear when Kelsey had walked up the length of it and pressed the door bell. Though this time she had to wait some minutes before her ring was answered. And the footsteps she heard when about to ring a fourth time were nothing like the light tapping of Yukiko, but were ponderous, almost stumbling, she thought.

But someone *was* coming! Excitement welled up in her again that soon she would see her father, the man she had not seen for four years—then Kelsey heard a crash as though the ponderous feet had knocked into something. And then the outer door, a sliding door, was being moved to one side in its grooves!

A smile was already breaking from her as the bent salt-and-pepper head started to lift from the door catch that seemed to have some interest for him. Kelsey was tall, about the same height as he was, but when her father raised his head, so her smile halted, and froze. As too, did the delighted cry of 'Dad!' that so nearly left her.

For this man was nothing like the man she had known. There was nothing in him to stir the memory of the laughing-eyed, invariably cheerful man who, when the mood was on him, would tease her and her mother unmercifully. His eyes glazed, he was stooping where never had he stooped before, and what was more, he was hanging on to the doorpost as if needing its support!

He's ill, was her first thought, her hands going forward to touch him, to help him, since he didn't look capable of standing unaided as hurried words of exclamation rushed to be heard.

But it was her father who spoke first. 'Kelsey!' he breathed harshly, as though seeing a ghost. 'Kelsey, ish—it you?'

The fumes from the spirits on his breath nearly knocked her back—and made her quickly revise her opinion that he was ill. Made her quickly realise that her father, a man who admittedly was not a teetotaller, was as high as a kite! Her father, a man who never drank to excess, was swaying in front of her eyes not because he was ill, but because he was drunk!

'Yes, Dad, it's me, Kelsey,' she said, sad to see him like this even as she took hold of his arms, not sure that he wasn't going to collapse. The unexpected sight of her on top of all he must have consumed being all too much for him.

But he did not want her assistance. And even plastered as he was, Kelsey had the evidence she wanted that he was still deeply in love with her mother. For, shaking off her hands and getting some sobriety from somewhere into his clouded brain, his first question as he attempted to stand upright was an eager:

'Has Eve come with you?'

Quickly, because that was the least painful way of doing it, Kelsey dashed his hopes. 'No,' she said, tears pricking the backs of her eyes that he seemed to crumple as this time he let her hands help him, 'I've come alone.'

That he accepted without question that she was there must, she thought as she helped him back inside, instinct turning his feet towards the sitting room, be all part of the stupor he was in.

Thinking he would be far better off in bed than where he was, she saw his glazed eyes search and rest on what little remained in the whisky bottle on the table next to him.

'I could do with a drink,' he slurred, a shaky hand going out to the bottle. And it was then that Kelsey discovered in her a hardness to his need she had not thought she possessed.

'I couldn't agree more,' she replied, and scooping up the bottle, on her way to hunt up the kitchen, 'I'll make you some coffee.'

It would take more than a gallon of black coffee to sober him up, she thought as she waited for the kettle to boil. But the hardness in her that had deprived him of another go at the whisky bottle had fast evaporated.

Oh, the dear, dear man! she mourned. Was this the result of her mother leaving him? Was it all down to his broken marriage that the oh, so proud man she had known should answer his front door in the state he was in?

Why, had not Yukiko been anxious to get back home, she too would have seen him—smelt his breath. And sober, if he was the man she had always thought him, he would have hated that.

She poured hot water into the beaker with the instant coffee, and fell to wondering what her mother would have thought if, as he had hoped, she had been with her. Even the hard front she had shown would have melted, Kelsey thought, and she then remembered the way, because of the love he had for his wife, something in her father's drink-befuddled brain had had him trying to shake off the effects of all he had consumed.

The coffee down him, he came out of his stupor, though he was still far from being sober. But she was glad to see some of his former pride was showing in that the first fairly coherent words she heard from him were a complaint of:

'You should have let me know you were coming.'

Belatedly, Kelsey agreed with him. 'I wanted to surprise you,' she said, her eyes gentle on him.

'You—did that all right,' he said, and it was his only reference to the state she had surprised him in.

Another beaker of black coffee, and he was asking, 'How did you find out where I live?' And rubbing a tired hand across his brow as he tried for memory, 'I'm certain I didn't write and tell your mother I'd moved.'

As far as Kelsey knew, he hadn't written at all. 'I called at your old address,' she explained, 'Yukiko Akita drove me over here.'

Henry Marchant thought about her reply for a few

ponderous moments. 'Yukiko's father and I work for the same firm,' he advised solemnly.

So, Kelsey guessed, the house where her parents used to live was still a company house. Her father worked somewhere high up in the export department of Forward Electronic, so very likely when he had told them that the house was too large, they had moved in Mr Akita and his family, and had found this smaller house for him.

She looked around the sitting room. It was square-shaped, though not all that small. It was furnished in Western style too, as also was what she could make out through the open sliding doors to be the bedroom.

Again she thought that bed was perhaps the best place for her father. But this time when possibly he might have accepted the suggestion, she saw, with him not watching every word he said, that she might be able to get more out of him than when sober, his pride might make him shut her out of anything he considered not her business.

'Why did you move into a smaller house, Dad?' she asked, thinking to go gradually until she got to the more crucial question of what had gone wrong between him and her mother.

'Why?' he asked, as if he was having difficulty in remembering. 'Why, because I couldn't afford to live there any more.'

If her mother was showing a decided stubbornness in refusing to so much as mention her husband by his first name, as much as by her determination not to return to Japan, then Kelsey found she had inherited a very stubborn streak herself too, in that she hadn't come all this way to be lied to or told to mind her own business. It was her business and, given that the pedestal she had placed her parents and their marriage on had crashed, she wanted it repaired and the two of them firmly up there again. So, intending to get to the very bottom of it, she probed deeper, playing along with the lie that he couldn't afford the rent of the bigger house when, accepting that he was making her mother a whacking allowance, she knew darn well he could.

'Can't afford it?' she queried, still looking for some signs of the man she remembered, a man who had never needed to resort to lying. 'What do you mean?' And bringing in her mother, the sooner to get the conversation flowing in the direction she wanted, 'I know you're making Mother a large allowance, but even if that leaves your wallet a little thinner, according to what Mother told me, you have quite a tidy nest egg saved.'

'Nest egg!' he repeated, and there was bitterness in his tone that was akin to the bitterness she had heard in her mother's voice, as he went on and shattered any idea she had that he had been lying when he had intimated that he was hard pressed. 'There is no *nest egg,* as you call it.'

'No ne . . .' Suddenly appalled, for surely he hadn't taken to gambling as well as drinking, Kelsey swallowed her fear that her mother's departure had sent him completely off the rails. She discovered that she hadn't heard the half of it as she pressed on to ask:

'You mean you've—spent your savings? That the money that was supposed to give you and Mother some comfort in your retirement has gone?'

Watching him, she saw pride trying to struggle through the weariness the effect of the Scotch he had drunk was having on him.

'Yes, it's gone,' he said, a shamed look she couldn't bear to see defeating the pride he was striving for. And, confessing the whole of it, 'Unwisely, I took the word of a man I thought I could trust above all others.' He seemed then to notice the sympathy in her face and he looked away from her as he told her, 'Had it not been for Serle Falconer insisting we were all on a winner, I would never have considered scraping every copper I could lay my hands on and making that investment.'

Investment! Kelsey hadn't a clue what he was talking about—but not being as befuddled as he was, she saw that there was only one way to find out more. 'The—er—investment failed?' she asked quietly, not taking her eyes from the man who was now evading looking at her. As yet she had no idea who Serle Falconer was either, though with a name like that she was certain that he wasn't Japanese.

'And how!' said Henry Marchant. 'All my money, every cent, all the money Eve and I had saved all these years, has gone down the drain.'

'Oh, Dad!' cried Kelsey, shocked. But she was to be far more shocked, as she watched, to see his face working and then crumple.

'And—d-down the drain with it went any chance I ever thought to have of me and E-Eve ever getting back together again.'

Horrified, Kelsey watched and saw her father, a man at the end of his tether, suddenly unable to take any more. Saw his humiliation complete, as he broke down totally.

'Oh, darling!' broke from her, and she was there beside him, her arms going round him, never ever expecting to see her father so utterly defeated and in tears. She shushed him, tears in her eyes too as she gently tried to make him feel better by telling him that he mustn't take it so badly, that this Serle Falconer must have lost a packet too.

'Not him,' he said, rubbing at his eyes as he tried to get himself together. 'He was strongly in favour of the investment, but it was only later that I heard, while shouting the odds about it being a chance of a lifetime, that he didn't risk one red cent of his own money.'

'You're saying that—that this man—urged you to take the risk when he knew all the time it was going to fail?' she asked incredulously, scandalised that her father so much as knew such a terrible person.

She saw him hesitate, but she knew it was only on

account of it not being his way to blacken another man's character. And not needing verbal confirmation to her question, she saved him the trouble of going against his nature.

'What sort of a man is he?' she asked indignantly, wondering how in the world her father, as canny as the next one, she had thought, should have been so persuaded by someone who obviously had the very glibbest of tongues.

'He's a man everybody trusts,' he replied, and choked, rubbing a hand across his eyes again, as his mind flitted back to the hopelessness of his ever getting together again with his beloved Eve. 'Oh, Kelsey,' he mourned, unable to check a stray tear, crucifying her that she should ever see him weep, 'It's all because of him that my marriage is irreparable. If it hadn't been for him—for my losing everything I possess—there might still have been a chance for your mother and me.'

Hugging him as he wept out his reasons for not joining her mother in England, Kelsey, sharing his heartbreak, experienced a surging hate for Serle Falconer. If the day ever came, she thought, when she and that snake in the grass Serle Falconer ever came face to face, then wouldn't she give him a piece of her mind! Wouldn't she just!

She found it almost unbearable that her father, struggling to find the backbone that had always been solid in him, should have gone so completely to pieces this way. God help Serle Falconer if she ever met up with him! she thought, wildly furious. If that day ever dawned, it would be touch and go that she wouldn't physically set about him!

CHAPTER TWO

KELSEY spent a fitful night, knowing it had nothing to do with her bed being a couple of fold-away mattresses on the thick *tatami* matting of the spare Japanese-style room she kept waking, for her bed was comfortable enough. But it was no wonder to her that she couldn't find rest; the sight of her weeping, worse-for-drink father and all he had told her had so shocked her, she wondered that she had been able to drop off at all.

Again she had that mental picture of him as he had been when, fearing that she was going to break down and weep with him, she had helped him into his bedroom. He had fallen asleep almost immediately, and would, she thought, be out for hours.

He had still been sound asleep when at ten that evening she had thought to investigate where she should sleep. And having found a spare room, having thought she was mind-weary enough from her thoughts to sleep the clock round, she too had gone to bed.

But sleep was far from her as light filtered into her room and she pondered the hopelessness of her father's position. And the hate that had sprung up for Serle Falconer rose up in her once more as she pieced together the fractured sentences her father had uttered.

Serle Falconer, on loan from Forward Electronic's subsidiary in England, was the only other European, or Westerner for that matter, working on the Japanese side. From what she could gather, this Serle Falconer was the bee's knees when it came to micro-electronics, and although wealthy in his own right, he had no need to work at all, his family having made a pile in property development or some such; according to her father his

26

first-class brain would have been wasted had he not chosen to work, and in the field he had.

Which was a pity, she thought angrily, that a first-class brain for micro-electronics should not go hand in hand with honesty. For no matter how garbled her father's version, it clearly boiled down to the fact that some know-it-all Englishman had persuaded him—though her father hadn't actually used that word 'persuaded'—to part with every penny he owned, in a worthless adventure which he himself had no intention of investing in.

She searched for some reason why such a man should deliberately lead her father on. But there was no answer, save that Serle Falconer must be some bigheaded, silky-tongued, careless swine, who had never bothered to give thought, when shouting the odds, that where he could afford to lose a packet without it hurting—though he hadn't lost a bean, had he?—to do so would cripple the man who, in her father's own words, trusted him above all other men.

She was on the point of going into the honesty-dishonesty angle of her summary and deciding that even if Serle Falconer—his very name made her see red!—had persuaded her father without thought to his financial position, it still made him dishonest in the light of the fact that *he* hadn't invested himself, when a sound made itself heard through the thin partitioning of her room.

It was still early yet, but that sound had her reaching for her robe, aware that with so much on his mind, now that the effects of the alcohol he had consumed had worn off, her father too was having difficulty in sleeping.

He had his back to her and was making himself a cup of coffee when silently by way of a net curtain that screened one side of her room, Kelsey vacated it.

'Can you make that two cups?' she asked, and felt pain spear through her when, startled, he spun round and she saw that, though sober now, he still looked terrible.

'I didn't dream it, then—you *are* here!'

And suddenly Kelsey was in the arms he stretched out to her. Then he was holding her at arm's length, his eyes searching her face, then away. And she knew then when he couldn't look at her that he was remembering the state in which she must have found him.

'You could do with a shave,' she said lightly to help him out, rubbing her chin that had come into contact with his bristles.

'Coffee first,' he replied, but her light comment had relaxed him, she saw. He spooned coffee into a second beaker, then as lightly as she had spoken, he queried, 'So how come you're here?'

It was a delicate moment. To say she had come to do what she could to get him and her mother back together again, their marriage repaired, when in the light of all he had told her it looked impossible—from his angle anyway—wouldn't, she saw, be of any help.

'I got fed up with my job and resigned,' she answered.

'Still as hotheaded as you always were?' he asked, seeming to know there had been nothing meek or mild about the way she had handed in her resignation.

'Who—me?' she exclaimed, remembering without regret her ex-employer's astonishment the last time she had let fly. 'Anyway,' she resumed, still keeping it light, 'I thought I'd come and pay you a surprise visit before I started looking for another job.'

'Some surprise!' he muttered. Then as he handed her a mug of coffee he did look her in the eye, bravely, she thought, because she could see he was ashamed. 'I'm sorry you found me the way you did. I—hm—don't often hit the bottle.'

Going gently, when he took a chair at the table, Kelsey followed suit, and slowly she said, 'Got too much for you, did it, love?'

He didn't answer, but took a long draught of his coffee. But suddenly, having got her question out for all it had gone unanswered, Kelsey knew that she wouldn't have a better opportunity than right now, regardless of how dreadful he was looking, to get it all out into the open. She was here to try and help, wasn't she? What help was she likely to be if they went around for the rest of her stay avoiding the issue?

She waited until he had put his coffee mug back down upon the table, then said quietly, 'I know that you're broke, Dad.'

His reply was instant and sharp, his head coming up abruptly. 'Who told you that?' And when she didn't immediately reply, he went to search into what he could remember of the conversation they must have had after she had arrived yesterday. 'Did I tell you I was broke?'

The poor lamb, she thought, wondering if he was going to try to deny it this morning. 'I know that the savings you were building up for your retirement went on an unsound investment,' she told him. And as the thought touched down that perhaps, without her knowing it, he had somehow been in direct communication with his wife, quickly she asked, 'Does Mother know?'

'Good God, *no!*' he exclaimed, horrified. And all at once he was a very stern parent, sterner than she had ever seen him, as heatedly he ordered, 'And don't you dare write and tell her!'

'But . . .' she tried to get in, only to have him snap:

'It's enough that I know what a bloody fool I've been, without Eve knowing it too!'

Heartbreakingly aware that not only did he love his wife, but that he still wanted to keep the respect she had shown for him throughout their married life, Kelsey knew it was too important an issue to let it go there, regardless of how annoyed or upset he was growing with her.

'But,' she insisted, 'I'm sure if you told her she would

understand.' And, rushing on when he looked as though he would jump down her throat, 'As it is, Mother thinks you won't leave here because your job is more important to you than she is. She doesn't know . . .' She broke off as a spasm of pain crossed his face. But it had cleared when, coming the heavy father again, he stressed sharply:

'I forbid you to tell her, Kelsey.' And when at his tone she just sat and looked dumbly, never having seen him like this before, he relented a little, and said, his voice softer, 'I know you love us both. But it isn't—just that.' And, suddenly confiding, maybe because he had nursed it to himself for too long, 'I don't know how much Eve has told you, but we were having a—few ups and downs before your phone call came calling her home.'

'But you've always got on so well,' Kelsey remembered—and heard then that there had been a lot kept back from her when, slowly, he revealed:

'Your mother had a bout of depression about a year ago,' and still hiding most of it, he settled for, 'It wasn't—an easy time.'

'You never wrote and . . .'

'We couldn't tell you. Gran had started to be ill, and I thought you had enough on your plate without worrying what was happening with us. Anyway,' he went on, 'Eve seemed to get better after a while, but I thought it would only send her off into depression again if she came home as she wanted to, to help you out. But she kept on and on about it, and I used the excuse of being too busy at work for not being able to go—for all our upsets, it never dawned on either of us then that she would go alone.'

That sounded so much like the parents she had always known that, even feeling weepy inside, Kelsey was able to offer an understanding smile.

'Meantime I began making enquiries into the possibility of my getting a job in England with a salary commensurate with my earnings here,' Henry Marchant resumed, but with a defeated look. 'I felt near to depression myself when I discovered that at fifty-three one is considered on the scrap-heap when applying for work. My chances of getting work in the UK, apparently, are nil.'

'But couldn't the firm you're with now help you out?' Kelsey asked eagerly. By the sound of it there was still a chance for her parents to get together again. 'I mean, they have a branch in England. You could . . .'

'Not a hope,' he flattened her by saying. 'Although the branch in England is a subsidiary of this one, they work entirely independently.' He thought for a moment, then said, 'There is a man here on loan from England, but then he's the head of the department, and pretty near indispensable to them.'

That man was Serle Falconer, she knew that. But she didn't want to think of him, it would make her angry. 'But you're high up too, aren't you?'

'Not *that* high up,' he replied. 'Besides, I'm on a contract that specifically states that if I leave the company in Japan before my contract is finished, then I sever all connection with Forward Electronic and its subsidiaries.'

'There must be some answer,' said Kelsey, having thought for some moments, but unable to come up with one.

'There isn't, love,' he replied sadly. 'If there was, I would have thought of it. I've spent days and days in thinking until my head hurt. I've sorted through a hundred different ways, all to no avail,' he said; no need for him now to hide that his dearest wish was to be reunited with his wife. 'But aside from our domestic differences, most of them because your mother wanted to see more of you,' he added, confirming what her mother had told her, 'what would we live on?'

The money he had so unwisely invested would have helped, she saw, anger in her against Serle Falconer

having her holding down her fury with him lest she
called him a few uncomplimentary names and took her
father away from the subject.

'What pension I've earned here will be frozen until I
reach retirement age,' he went on when she had no
answer for him of what could he live on if he returned
to England. 'As will the frozen pension I have from the
job I had before I took this one.'

And as Kelsey went back to damning Serle Falconer
and his persuasive tongue, Henry Marchant sighed and
brought out the name of the man she was learning to
hate more with every passing minute.

'I was near to being desperate on the day your
mother left,' he told her. 'I just knew that she wouldn't
be coming back. But it was when I saw Serle Falconer
at Komatsu airport, taking the same Tokyo-bound
plane as your mother, that I just knew he was jetting off
to Tokyo in order to raise all the spare cash he could to
make a massive investment of his own.'

'But that wasn't his reason for going?' she asked,
knowing the answer before sadly he shook his head,
then continued:

'I couldn't take that it might be years until I saw Eve
again, so back in my office I reasoned that if the
investment was as good as it had to be with Serle
dropping everything to go to Tokyo, then if I invested
too I stood to make more than enough for me to follow
her very soon.'

Kelsey was right there with him in his thinking, and
sad though it was, she could quite well understand his
reasons for throwing his usual caution to the wind.
Though had it not been for that treacherous Falconer,
he would never have acted so rashly.

But her father was going on, and again she found
herself biting down the vitriolic remarks which would
have let him know just what she thought of the man
who, after what he had done, he could still call by his
first name.

'I wanted to give Eve as much spare cash as I could, in the rushed circumstances, so I paid her flight by credit card. I didn't want her to have to worry about money on top of everything else that awaited her in England,' he explained. 'Anyway,' he went on, getting back to the investment, 'my credit is good, and I had little trouble in getting a loan from my bank to add to the amount I've saved all these years.'

Oh lord, she thought, it was much worse than she had thought. 'So you invested the whole lot?' she asked, her face fallen into the same unhappy lines as his.

He nodded. 'So you see, Kelsey, even if I threw my hand in here and was able to find a job in England—which I very much doubt—I still wouldn't be able to leave.' And showing what a very honourable man he was, he ended, 'There's no chance of me going anywhere until I've settled all my debts here.'

Which fully explained, she thought when, shaven and looking very much better than he had first thing, he went off to his office, why he had moved into a smaller house with a smaller monthly rental. Insisting as he was on sending her mother that hefty monthly allowance so she should not know that anything was wrong, he was doing all he could to not only survive, but to pay something off the heavy debts that were weighing him down.

Her thoughts that day, as she set about cleaning up a house that was sorely in need of a woman's touch, were a mixture of utter sadness for her parents and the impossibility of her attempt to bring them together; and anger that boiled up in her at the thought of Serle Falconer who had led her father into the terrible plight he was in.

A telephone call from Yukiko Akita gave her a little respite from sadness and anger, Yukiko explaining that she would not be able to call on her for a few days as she and her parents were rather busy. That Yukiko was sounding rather mysterious must be from her translating her thoughts from Japanese into English, Kelsey thought.

'But perhaps,' said Yukiko, a hidden excitement coming through in her voice, 'I may see you on Friday?'

'I would like that,' answered Kelsey, much as she had before, and put the phone down to go back to anguished thoughts of her father.

Why, even the nest egg had gone, she grieved, growing fairly certain then that had her father not been in debt up to his ears, missing her mother as he did, then if he had still had his savings, that ache for her would have made him throw a different caution to the winds, and break his contract and take the risk on being able to find a job in England.

He was much brighter when he returned home that evening. Not that he fooled her for a minute by the chatty way he was with her. But if he was putting a bright face on it just because she was there, then it was the least she could do to meet him halfway. Though for all that, there were a few occasions throughout that evening when, forgetful that she was there, he would let a desolate look come over his face.

Having told him of Yukiko's friendly phone call, Kelsey then had to re-tell him, since he couldn't remember her telling him before, that it had been Yukiko who had driven her over yesterday, hastily tacking on that Yukiko had offered apologies for not being able to stay to say 'Hello'. Which made him embarrassed at the way he had been yesterday, and covering it by telling her, 'Yukiko's father works at Forward Electronics too,' news he had already imparted.

Kelsey went to bed that night wondering what else he had forgotten he had told her. And thinking of his embarrassment, his shame at her finding him in his cups, for his pride's sake, she resolved never to mention the day of her arrival again.

But it was in conversation with him the following evening, having told him she had used 'Gran's money' to make the trip, that when he asked her how long she could stay, Kelsey discovered that where her mother was concerned, his pride was as great as ever as, honestly, she told him:

'I had hoped you might somehow be able to travel back with me.' And at the shake of his head, 'Or failing that,' though she didn't want to admit failure, 'that I'd stay on a while. But it's been going through my mind since that it might be better for me to give you the money I've brought to last me my stay and to take a cheap flight home.'

'No!' His answer was instant and sharp. 'Apart from what money you have being money your grandmother wanted you to have, it wouldn't come anywhere near to settling my debts. Besides which, I'm not having your mother wondering why you've returned so suddenly— and penniless.' And having delivered his lecture, he smiled suddenly and said, 'Anyhow, I want to see something of you myself.'

By the time Friday came around, Kelsey had the little one-storied home looking spick and span. She had written to her mother, but, unable to enter fully into the deception her father was practising, she had refrained from putting any address at the top of her notepaper. If her mother did reply, she thought she could laugh off any awkwardness when Yukiko passed her letter over, by saying her mother must automatically have put the old address on the envelope.

Having strolled to the village shops several times, she was now used to seeing fields of rice growing along the sides of the road, and had looked her fill at various shaped and sized houses, discovering different routes to and from the bungalow she now called home, passing shrines and monuments on her way.

Yukiko had telephoned yesterday to suggest that if Kelsey would like to do some shopping, she would be pleased to go with her, when they could look round the shopping area in Doihara-machi.

So that Friday morning Kelsey made light work of tidying up the house after her father had gone to his office, and she was ready and waiting when she heard the Honda pull up.

In the absence of the wheat tea the Japanese girl had offered when she had invited her into her home, Kelsey offered Yukiko coffee. And in town, having visited every floor of the Seiyu department store, it was on the eighth and final floor of that building that Yukiko suggested Kelsey might like to rest while they had another coffee.

By this time, after polite beginnings, Kelsey and Yukiko were getting on famously. And over coffee in the small but cosy café type restaurant, Yukiko revealed that the mystery Kelsey had felt in the other's voice on Monday was not from any translation difficulty, but stemmed from Yukiko being excited because she and her parents had been busy with negotiations concerning her probable forthcoming marriage.

'Probable?' queried Kelsey, happy for Yukiko, but puzzled since in her view one was either going to be married or one was not.

'The go-between was going to call on Tuesday, but then because of some family illness, he had to put it off to Wednesday,' said Yukiko, as though that explained everything.

'Go-between?'

'You do not have such people in England?' Yukiko queried in return. And at Kelsey's shake of her head, she went on to explain that after having seen her photograph, a certain man had desired to meet her. A go-between had then brought the man's photograph for her parents to see, and after the go-between had revealed the man's history, his social position and so on, her parents had shown her the man's picture and had asked her if she wished to see him. A formal meeting had then taken place between the man with his parents present, and Yukiko, traditionally dressed in a kimono, and with her parents present, and for two months now she had been 'walking out' with the young man in question. On Wednesday last, the go-between had come to her parents to ask if the young man could have Yukiko's hand in marriage, and tonight the go-between would ask her father for his answer.

'The go-between is going to ask your *father* if you'll marry this young man?' Kelsey questioned, blinking.

'That is right,' replied Yukiko happily.

Hiding her astonishment, Kelsey knew such a way of going on would never do for her. When she met and married, she knew it would be to a man she had met independently. Someone whom she had met and fallen in love with without someone bringing her a photograph of some man she had never met, but who was interested in her. She wanted that same spontaneous love her parents had found—she would settle for nothing less.

'Is there always a go-between?' she thought to ask.

'Oh yes,' beamed Yukiko.

'But if you do not want to marry this man, you can say no,' pressed Kelsey, thinking, while able to accept that their cultures were different, that it would be appalling if one had to marry against one's own inclination.

'Yes, I can,' replied Yukiko. Though she qualified, 'But if my father thinks I should marry the man, he can say yes for me even if I do not wish it.'

How dreadful, Kelsey thought, though seeing Yukiko was still beaming happily, she said, 'But you do wish to say yes?' Her reply was another excited beaming smile. Though when Kelsey followed up and said, 'And your father knows this?' suddenly Yukiko's smile began to fade, and all at once she was looking quite anxious.

Quickly then she consulted her watch. Then, looking a shade agitatedly at her companion, she said, 'I did not see my father before he left for work this morning. I

know he has a long meeting this afternoon when I will
not be able to see him.' And, unable to hide her
agitation as she glanced at Kelsey's by now empty
coffee cup and stood up. 'I am certain he knows my
answer is yes, but I must go and see him in case he has
got it wrong.'

Obviously, Kelsey realised, she had thoughtlessly put
a doubt in the other girl's mind. But try as she would to
put the matter right, Yukiko would not rest until she
had seen her father.

Back in the car, driving along in the direction for
Forward Electronic as fast as the traffic would allow,
Yukiko recovered some of her composure sufficiently to
suggest that she would introduce Kelsey to her father.
But seeing that the discussion Yukiko wanted with her
parent was a very private one, regretting as she was
having put the doubt in Yukiko's mind, Kelsey told her
that since her own father worked at Forward Electronic
perhaps it might be in order if she paid him a visit.

'Of course,' replied Yukiko straight away, having by
now travelled some miles and pulling into the gates of a
vast factory area. 'What am I thinking of? I had
forgotten for the moment that Marchant-*san* works
here too.'

Kelsey smiled in understanding as Yukiko took her
to one of the buildings that housed many offices, and
showed her the door to Henry Marchant's office, before
turning with some speed to go in search of her own
parent.

Sure Yukiko's anxieties would soon be relieved,
Kelsey allowed herself a small smile as she visualised
her father's surprised expression when he saw her.

At first she thought to knock. Then with the thought
of making it a bigger surprise—he thought she was
swanning around shopping—very quietly she opened
the door Yukiko had pointed out. Silently she pushed
the door forward—then stopped dead, a welter of
sadness choking her.

For her suspicions that her father's brightness all this week was solely a face he was putting on because she was there were abruptly borne out. Shaken by the grief in the face of the man sitting staring into space, entirely unaware that anyone had so silently come in, Kelsey felt too stunned to move.

Then, as quietly as she had stepped across the threshold, she backed out, carefully closing the door behind her. Her heart was anguished as the picture of her father stayed with her, the work before him ignored, a look of such pain in him that it had been too unbearable for her to stay and watch.

Oh, Dad, oh love, she fretted, unable to get the image of the stark naked hurt in him from her. Had he remembered the tears she had seen him shed, he would have been ashamed. But those tears were as nothing when compared to that lost-to-the-world, haunted expression on his face. Her father wasn't just crying inside—he was bleeding!

How long she stood there leaning against the wall, unaware she had moved nearer the wall needing its support, Kelsey didn't know. But her mind and heart were still with her father when she saw a tall man leave one of the offices up ahead and, with never a look in her direction, go further up the corridor where he disappeared into another office.

Quite when the consciousness hit her that the man she had just vaguely seen was not Japanese but was European, she wasn't sure. But when remembrance got through the deep sorrow she was feeling, memory coming of her father saying that the only other European working for Forward Electronic was Serle Falconer, Kelsey straightened away from the wall.

That swine—that swine of a man was responsible for her father looking as if the emotions in him were too much to bear, she thought. And as searing rage exploded in her, Kelsey had to think no further. In five seconds flat she had charged up the corridor and was outside the door she had seen the tall European go through.

And this was another door she didn't knock at either. Without stopping to think that it might not be Serle Falconer's office, or that he could be having a meeting, or anything else, she was storming through the door and was immediately facing the brown-haired man who looked up as she crashed into what must be his office, since he was alone and sitting behind the desk it housed.

Studious blue eyes looked back at her from a broad-shouldered man somewhere in his mid-thirties. But Kelsey wasn't bothered what his age was. She had just seen her father emotionally crippled, and it was all due to *him!*

'Are you Falconer?' she challenged rudely, the fire of temper showing in her sizzling brown eyes.

'None other,' he replied, looking cool where she was a furnace of fury, his eyes appraising her slender figure, filing away, and spending time on her shapely mouth before he met the fury in her eyes again. 'Forgive me, but your name escapes me for the moment.'

At any other time, his detached air, his pulling her up short that she should blaze her way into his office when they had not so much as been introduced, might have had her faltering. But having come from a despair of her own to see her father so patently distressed, and Falconer the cause, nothing he could say then would have detracted her from her arm.

'You louse!' she shot at him. 'You unmitigated louse!' And uncaring that though he still looked cool on the surface his eyes had narrowed at the way she was insulting him, she rushed on, 'How with all you have on your conscience you can calmly sit there . . .'

She broke off. She had known he was tall, from a distance she had seen that much. But at her charge of how he could calmly sit there, Serle Falconer, unhurried and with eyes still narrowed, slowly rose to his feet.

And it was the way, ominously quietly, that he came round his desk and, tall though she was, towered over her, that told her that here was a man it would be most unwise to cross. Why, she thought, for the moment flummoxed, as mad as she was with him, just the fact that he had moved made her speech dry up!

But she wasn't afraid of him. He had hurt her father—through his persuasive tongue he had hurt her mother too—and anger was storming through her again as she told herself he couldn't hurt her any more than, through her parents' unhappiness, she had been hurt already.

CHAPTER THREE

'WHAT—did you call me?' Serle Falconer asked, just as though he hadn't heard her the first time. Just as though, Kelsey thought, he was daring her to repeat it.

'You heard!' she blazed, refusing to let it worry her that he looked capable of throwing her from the room without bothering to open the door if she said it again. 'I called you a louse,' she repeated unflinchingly, 'and in my book, that is exactly what you are!'

Those narrowed blue eyes that this close she saw held an icy look—which contrasted oddly with that crooked curve still on his mouth—took on a warmer look as he surveyed her furious expression, and noted that she was nowhere near backing down.

And then suddenly that warmer look in his eyes changed to what, if she wasn't mistaken, was pure and utter devilment. And far from throwing her head first from his office, he was all at once rocking back on his heels, still unaware of her identity, and again asking her forgiveness as he went on to needle her into telling him who she was.

'Forgive me,' he said, his face now solemn, that curve gone from his mouth, 'didn't the paternity allowance come through?'

'What?' Her anger abated as she tried to catch up.

'You're as mad as hell about something,' he replied smoothly. 'And though I can't remember every female who's—er—passed my way, if you'll give me a hint of what I called you the last time we met, I'll try to remem . . .'

Fury filled her at his intimation that they had once lain together, and that it was so insignificant to him that he had forgotten her.

42

'Why, you . . .' she cut him off furiously before she could take a grip on herself. 'My name is Kelsey Marchant and we have never . . .' His self-satisfied smile halted the word 'met'.

'I didn't think we had.' He cut her off this time, deliberately misinterpreting her, she knew, as he added, 'I didn't think my memory was so bad that I would have forgotten having anyone as shapely as you in my arms.'

'Cut it out!' she snapped aggressively, not caring that his eyes had gone chilly again at her bossing him around; she hadn't come here to be baited but to give him a piece of her mind. 'I'm Henry Marchant's daughter and . . .'

'That much I'd gathered,' he drawled.

'I arrived in Komatsu last Sunday,' she ignored him, 'and . . .'

'Hardly long enough, I see, for the pretty manners of Japanese girls to rub off on you,' he interrupted urbanely.

'And found my father a shadow of his former self,' she pressed on, feeling far from docile as she imagined he thought her Japanese counterpart would be.

'Rather a dramatic way of putting it,' Serle Falconer dropped laconically, doing nothing to quieten her anger by his choice of words. But, serious all of a sudden, he commented thoughtfully, 'Though come to think of it, I seem to remember Henry looking a shade off colour the other day when . . .'

'A shade off colour!' Kelsey exploded. Why, her father was nothing like the man who had visited England four years previously. 'He's worried to death,' she said tartly, her brown eyes glaring at the man who was ultimately responsible for her father's worries. 'And it's all your fault!'

'*My* fault?' That took him aback, she saw. And there was not a smile or a hint of mockery there, when sharply Serle Falconer charged, 'What the hell have I got to do with the way your father is looking?'

'You're trying to make me believe you don't know?' she sneered contemptuously.

'So tell me,' he ordered flatly. And that angered her further, because he knew, of course he knew.

'You know damn well what I'm talking about!' she flared, and when he just stared without speaking, his eyes icy on her, his face as stern as ever she had seen her father's, anger that he was still insisting on this pretence had her fairly spitting at him, 'You know damn well that my father trusts your word over any man's, yet that didn't stop you from persuading him to invest his life's savings in stock you knew full well to be worthless!'

'Invest . . .' For the first time she seemed to be getting through. But she had to own that Falconer was a first-class actor, that he actually managed to look incredulous just as though his brain was ticking over and that it had just clicked which stock her father had so unwisely invested in. Then, 'My God,' he said, looking staggered, 'Henry never put his money in . . .'

'Why wouldn't he?' she challenged hotly. 'You'd told him there was a killing to be made.'

'Because Henry never invests in stock,' she was coldly told. 'There have been other deals when any business man would need his head examining not to invest, yet your father never touched any of them.'

'Then you must have been more persuasive than usual over this one,' Kelsey spat at him.

And the way she was then, Serle Falconer could have tried telling her he'd had nothing to do with her father losing his all until he was blue in the face and she wouldn't believe him. It showed in her face as she reviled him.

'When I called you a louse, Serle Falconer, I meant it!' she snapped, and her chin thrust forward aggressively at the harshness that had come over him. 'Though in my view, louse is too good a name for you!'

As angry as she was, it irked her that he just stood there and made no attempt to excuse his persuasive tongue. Irked her, and egged her on to want some sign from him that he was remorseful.

'But it doesn't matter a fig to you that my father is broke, does it?' she challenged. 'You're sitting comfy-cosy, aren't you, Mr Shout-the-odds-Falconer!'

Some small satisfaction came to her that his face hardened, but he still wasn't making excuses, although it looked as though he wanted to shut her up.

'You from your wealthy background,' she jibed, refusing to shut up. 'You don't care that much,' she flicked her fingers in front of his face, 'that my father . . .'

It came then, the fracture in the armour that she had been looking for. 'Enough,' he rapped. 'Be quiet!'

'Why should I be quiet?' she shrieked. 'You can afford to take a loss! My father is in debt through you. If you hadn't . . .'

'I said that's enough,' he threatened.

Kelsey ignored his threat. 'Call yourself a gentleman!' she scorned. 'I haven't started on the substitute names I have for . . .'

It was as far as she got. To feel that mouth she had had to admit attractive over hers, to feel strong muscled arms around her—arms there was no breaking away from—was something totally unexpected. And the anger in her went absolutely wild as she struggled furiously to try to get away from him, pushed and pummelled at him to try and break his kiss.

And at last she managed it. Even if a little voice inside her head did give the opinion that she was free only because Serle Falconer decreed it.

But as he took a pace back from her, and she saw that mocking satisfaction in his face that where his order to be quiet had not been effective, he had effectively silenced her by another method, for speechlessly she was staring at him, so all hell broke loose inside her. And even as she was thinking that perhaps she had gone a bit over the top in trying to get some reaction from him, so blinding rage consumed her; and her hand went streaking through the air and caught him a blow he must surely have been expecting, although he did nothing to stop it.

Her hand stung as it dropped to her side, but even as his head jerked to one side from the force of her blow, she saw he still had that mocking look in his eyes as he said:

'That round, I think, was even. Shall we retire to neutral corners before we come out for the next one?'

'Eat your heart out, Falconer,' she snapped at him viciously. 'Having seen you once is sufficient for me!'

Mockingly he considered her, then softly he drawled, 'Strange though it may seem, I wasn't asking you for a date.'

'Which is just as well,' she flared, wanting to hit him again as she saw him smile, but having to go on even though she knew he was aware he had succeeded in needling her, 'because you're the very last man I would consider going out with!'

'Which means,' he came back, not a bit put out, 'that you may have rather a dull time during your stay.'

'Meaning you're the only *personable* bachelor around here?' Kelsey queried, her tone letting him know that his idea of personable and hers were very different.

'Meaning you'd better de-fluff that bit of shelf,' he said loftily. 'There's going to be no chance of you getting off it while you're in these parts.'

Utterly infuriated by his snide suggestion that she was on the look-out for a husband, she knew darn well, with him being the sole eligible european locally, that he was only trying to get a rise out of her by intimating that she could die an old maid before he would contemplate marrying her. And, aware that it was not unknown for a Western girl to marry a Japanese man, Kelsey had to wonder what on earth had got into her that, having told him what she thought of him, she was staying to bandy words with this man.

'You should get to be so lucky,' she tossed acidly. 'When I marry it will be to a man I love!'

As she paused for breath, he mocked softly:

'Well, well, the lady's a romantic!'

Aware too late that she had revealed more to this astute man than she had intended, she knew her only defence was attack. 'And what's wrong with that?' she challenged. 'What's wrong with anyone wanting a love that's born on the first spontaneous meeting?'

'You have your parents in mind?'

Astute wasn't the word for him, Kelsey thought. But she stayed to answer him then purely because it was important that neither he nor anyone else knew the present state of her parents' marriage.

'Their marriage is perfect,' she answered, her chin tilting defiantly, daring him to contradict her.

'I've always thought so myself,' he agreed, when she had thought they would never agree on anything. But he spoilt the picture she was trying to convey, deliberately, she thought, when he added shrewdly, 'Though what happens behind closed doors is anybody's guess.' And, 'Did your mother come to Japan with you, by the way?' he asked.

'I assure you,' said Kelsey, determined to leave no room for speculation, what with Falconer being British too, knowing that any matter appertaining to her grandmother's estate could be dealt with by phone and letter, no need for her mother, having already been in England for three months, not to have come back with her, 'that there is nothing at all the matter with my parents' marriage.'

'I'm glad to hear it,' he replied.

But as she walked to the door, intending to leave him without another word, so Kelsey found him right there with her, his hand going to the door handle and preventing her from opening it. Wondering what he had to say now, she turned to look at him, and didn't trust at all that sardonic look on his face. She suspected that whatever it was he had to say, it would not be without a sting in its tail—she was not mistaken.

'Before you leave may I wish you joy in finding the love of your life—the man of your life,' he amended pleasantly. Kelsey thanked him for nothing, and was glad she had remained silent when, his words matching his sardonic look, he added, 'But if all else fails, there's always *Omiai*.'

'*Omiai?*' she queried, knowing she should be knocking his hand from the door handle and opening the door herself.

'*Miai-kekkon*—an arranged marriage,' he mocked. Then, his tone toughening, 'Few men would put up with a little termagant like you who steams in to hurl accusations before she knows the full facts.' But the mockery was back as he taunted, 'Yes, *Omiai* might well be the answer to your pray . . .'

'Go to hell!' Kelsey cut in, knowing very well she knew all the facts if he was referring to the way he had persuaded her father to make a worthless investment. 'I would never,' she added vehemently to put him right, '*never* stand for an arranged marriage!' And having put him right, 'Though with that shelf *you're* perched up on getting clogged thick with dust, *Omiai* might be the only way for you to get any girl to have you!'

That she had somehow tickled his sense of humour with her parting shot, for that had been a definite laugh she had heard as the door closed, further annoyed Kelsey. Swine! she thought, but she had to take the cross look from her face, because Yukiko had just turned into the corridor, and from the happy look of her, all was once more all right with her world.

'You have seen your father?' Yukiko asked at once.

'More to the point, have you seen yours?' she evaded,

too late now to knock first and then go into her father's office. Yukiko would only wonder where she had been all this time—some instinct told Kelsey that Serle Falconer would not breathe a word of her visit, or of her father being broke, to anyone. Though why she knew that she couldn't have said, other than perhaps it wouldn't show Falconer up in a very good light if he did noise it around and it came out that it was throught his advice that her father was on his uppers.

Beaming again, Yukiko forgot she had asked a question, 'My father understood my wishes all the time,' she replied. 'I think perhaps I am a little over-anxious at the present time.'

That evening when Henry Marchant returned from work, Kelsey took one look at his face and decided against telling him anything of her visit to Forward Electronic. She had witnessed for herself only that very morning how despairing he was, and she wasn't surprised that that night, unlike every other evening this week, the effort to appear bright and cheerful seemed just too much for him.

Throughout the weekend that followed, she did her best to bring him out of the slough of despondency in which he had fallen, but without success. So that by the time he left for work on Monday morning, she was altering her opinion that she had perhaps gone a little over the top where Serle Falconer was concerned. She recalled how her hand had stung after that blow she had struck him, but she found only small comfort in that. All she could hope for was that if ever she did meet him again, the chance might present itself to hit him harder.

Towards mid-morning Yukiko telephoned, and the bubbling happiness in her that came through was all Kelsey needed to tell her that, though she personally found the idea of an arranged marriage appalling, Yukiko was overjoyed at the prospect.

'Your father's meeting went well on Friday?' she

asked, knowing Yukiko would know she wasn't talking of the lengthy meeting she had spoken of his having with his business colleagues.

'Exceptionally well,' bubbled Yukiko. 'I am to be married in four months' time!'

In the face of Yukiko's sublime happiness at the prospect, Kelsey squashed her feelings that it would never do for her, and gave Yukiko her warm congratulations—then heard that the Japanese girl had a hundred and one things to do that day, but that she would be so pleased if Kelsey could spare time from her day tomorrow.

'Perhaps we can lunch together?' Yukiko queried. 'Maybe you would like to see an authentic Japanese restaurant that has not been Westernised?'

'I would, very much,' Kelsey said eagerly, and replaced the phone having arranged for Yukiko to call at twelve the following day.

That night Henry Marchant was as depressed as he had been all weekend, hitting on the head her theory that perhaps the company of his male colleagues during the day might take him out of himself.

'I'm lunching with Yukiko tomorrow, she telephoned this morning,' Kelsey told him during the evening.

'She's a nice girl,' he commented.

'Yukiko got engaged at the weekend,' she thought to tell him, anything to get his mind off his thoughts, which she didn't need any telling were not in Japan but with his adored Eve in England.

His grunt for an answer was sufficient to tell her that she wasn't making much of a job of directing this thoughts into happier channels.

'It's an arranged marriage, I think,' she pressed on, and saw she had gained enough of his attention for him to tell her:

'That's not unusual out here.'

Refraining from putting forward her own views lest it sent him off to remember his own spontaneous joyous meeting with the girl who later became his wife, having got his attention, Kelsey expressed an interest she didn't feel in *miai-kekkon*, and Henry Marchant was coming away from his thoughts and was telling her that many Japanese girls, when they reached the age of twenty, had photographs taken of themselves dressed in a kimono, so as to be ready for when such time arrived as the *Nakōdo*, the go-between, required a photograph to take to the parents who had requested the *Nakōdo* to find a good girl for their son.

'You mean he takes the girl's photo without her having any idea who the son is?' she asked, remembering Yukiko telling her she had received her fiancé's photograph *after* he had seen hers, forgetting completely, as her eyes flew wide, that this had started out as an exercise to lift her father from his despair.

'Not only that,' she was told, 'but before it gets that far, the go-between will have asked around locally into the girl's character, and into the mental and physical health of her family. It's a system that on the whole works quite well.'

Having got him talking, Kelsey went to her room that night pleased he had been lifted a little from his depression. For he had spoken at some length about the way a good number of Japanese found their life's partner, and not only had she learned a little more, but she had also learned that he even seemed to think the system held quite a few merits!

Perhaps it was because he had spent so many years in Japan that he appeared to see the old custom quite acceptable, she thought. But that did not stop her independent spirit from thinking no matter how long she stayed in Japan, for herself, she would *never* find it acceptable.

Thinking of how long she should stay in Japan gave food for other thought before she fell asleep. Should she, she pondered, soon start making noises about going home? Sleep claimed her as she was thinking that with her father so down, not to mention the plight he was in, she didn't really see how at the moment she could possibly leave.

The restaurant Yukiko took her to the next day was a pure delight to Kelsey. As restaurants went, it was a fairly small affair. But she loved the cosy look where low tables on a platform formed a U-shape, and where, following Yukiko's example, she had to step down to shed her shoes, then follow the kimono-attired waitress to step up again to their table. Again copying Yukiko, she sat with her legs bent to the side of her as they sat on cushions, leaving it to her new friend to do the ordering.

'*Arigatō,*' she thanked the waitress, trying out her smattering of Japanese when a handleless cup filled with green tea was placed before her.

The meal, when it came, was presented all on the same tray, so that soup, rice and *tempura*—fish, shellfish and vegetables deep-fried in a light batter— were eaten as one fancied, as far as she could gather; with a drink of soup interspersed with the main course.

It was during their meal that Kelsey spotted the diamond ring adorning Yukiko's engagement finger. 'Yukiko, how beautiful!' she exclaimed, and Yukiko extended her delicately shaped hand for her to get a closer look.

'A new custom,' giggled Yukiko a shade selfconsciously. 'But one I like very much,' she said, going on to tell Kelsey how yesterday she had gone with her fiancé to select it.

Talk over their lunch was lighthearted, with the waitress moving silently near on her *tabi*-clad feet, *tabi* being a firm-soled type of sock with the cotton upper divided at the big toe to allow thonged shoes to be worn for outdoor wear.

When the meal was over, Kelsey went with Yukiko to where they had left their shoes. And for the moment she felt happy, rich in the experience of her first real taste of Japan, a smile hovering at the corners of her mouth.

But when, as she was straightening from donning her footwear her eyes progressed upwards, past the lightweight suiting of the man standing on the small platform waiting for her to get out of the way so he could occupy her small space and shed his shoes, and on upwards, a particularly tall Japanese, she was thinking, Kelsey's smile abruptly disappeared. For the man was not Japanese at all, and her eyes were meeting full on the blue eyes of the man who had laughed at her the last time she had seen him.

Her pleasure spoilt, no thought in her but to look through him, her only idea was to ignore him. But then it was she discovered that Yukiko, having seen and recognised Serle Falconer too, was now bowing in greeting not only to him but to the two business-suited Japanese companions he had with him.

Tight-lipped, Kelsey would have stepped onto the platform and pushed past him if he didn't get out of the way. But he had observed that, the swine, she thought, and not only that, she found, for it seemed that he was hell bent on having another laugh at her expense.

'Aren't you going to introduce me to your friend, Yukiko-*san*?' she heard him ask pleasantly. And blocked as she was because his two companions had moved closer to him, and short of barging through the three of them there was no way she was going to get by, Kelsey had to stand fuming as Yukiko straight away rushed into apologising charmingly for her lack of manners in not introducing her.

'My apologies, Falconer-*san*. May I introduce Miss Kelsey Marchant. Kelsey-*san* is Marchant-*san*'s daughter who is honouring us with a visit.' And turning to Kelsey, 'This is . . .'

Kelsey stopped her right there. She could, she considered, have kept their war private, but why should she! If he thought she was meekly going to shake hands with him when it was he who had been instrumental in bringing about her father's financial ruin, then did he have another think coming! So, chopping off Yukiko before she could get any further with her introduction, Kelsey ignored the large hand that confidently started to extend to her, and throwing him a withering look, and putting every ounce of contempt of which she was capable into her voice, she announced coldly for anyone caring to listen:

'I am very particular with whom I shake hands.' And going on doggedly, not missing the ice forming in narrowed eyes, 'And never would I consider shaking hands with someone I would not trust further than I could see them.'

An appalled silence followed her contemptuous little speech, as in an instant the smooth urbanity of Serle Falconer, like his outstretched hand, fell away. And in that instant of his expression changing to one of murderous fury, Kelsey knew that in the polite society of Japan, not only did Falconer know himself blatantly insulted, but his companions knew it too.

For a moment, as rage she couldn't miss burned fiercely in his blue eyes, Kelsey thought she was going to be on the receiving end of that same head-jerking slap she had served him. But as suddenly as his jaw clenched, so she saw he had his fury under control. Though while she did not feel intimidated that he looked set to knock her head from her shoulders—instinct telling her he wouldn't set about her in public—it was what replaced that look of white-hot fury that set her nerves tingling and had her wondering if perhaps she had gone a little too far. For there was now an ominous threat in those eyes that had darkened, eyes which were refusing to let hers go. And while it could not have lasted more than a few seconds, she read a clear message there, a threatening message as those narrowed eyes looked menacingly back at her—and that message as clear as day was telling her, 'Nobody publicly insults me and gets away with it. I'll sort you somehow, Kelsey Marchant—count on it!'

Kelsey blinked, and the next time she looked at him, that smooth urbanity was back. And she was then left wondering as he stood politely to one side and she stepped up and past him—had she read in his eyes what she had thought she had read?

With Yukiko right behind her, Kelsey pushed her head in the air and marched from the restaurant. But not before she heard Serle Falconer say something in Japanese to his companions, and not before she heard all three of them burst out laughing at what he had said.

But when, reaching the Honda, she turned to Yukiko to try and make some apology if she had made her feel uncomfortable back there, she saw that Yukiko was not a bit put out, but was smiling happily as if she had heard what that swine Falconer had said and that it had amused her too.

'What did Falconer say?' she asked, her apology to Yukiko forgotten in the face of its looking as though everybody was having a good laugh at her expense. Though of course she might just be being over-sensitive about anything connected with that damned man.

'Falconer-*san* say,' replied Yukiko, accepting Kelsey's use of his surname as though thinking she was copying the Japanese way, but had forgotten to add *'san'* at the end; this being borne out when she retold what he had said, 'that you are trying to pick up the pretty manners of Japanese girls, and instead of wanting to shake hands on introduction, you wish to bow only instead.'

The names Kelsey reserved for Serle Falconer were released with a vengeance once Yukiko had dropped her off, and she was within the privacy of the bungalow.

Cocky devil, she fumed, certain she hadn't bowed to him. Though trust him to come up with that for an answer for her cutting him. He had even turned the fact that—now she recalled it—she *had* bent her head, but only to see where she was going when she had stepped up on to that platform in order to leave the restaurant.

For the rest of the time at her disposal until her father came home, Kelsey railed against Serle Falconer and the fact that for a second time he had had a laugh at her expense. But at other times when her mutiny against him waned, she was left to remember that cold chilly threat in his eyes that said that somehow, somewhere, he was going to get even with her.

She wondered if perhaps by turning the fact it looked as though she had bowed to his advantage, he now thought the debt square. But try as she might to forget that 'You just wait, my lady!' look in his eyes, Kelsey found that she could not. Somehow, she had a dreadful suspicion that Serle Falconer was the sort of man who never forgot an insult, and that when he went after his pound of flesh, he would not settle for less. Though what else he could do that was more diabolical than what he had done already, she could not begin to think.

On that thought, she finally ejected Serle Falconer and his look of enraged fury from her mind. It was just not possible, she thought, for him to cap what he had already done—so she had no need to give him another moment's thought.

Though after their meal that night, and with her father in the same dark mood as he had been the night previously before she had got him talking, Kelsey searched around in her head for a subject which might take him out of himself.

'You haven't asked me how I got on with my first Japanese meal,' she said in an attempt to tease.

'Neither I did,' he replied, for her sake trying to lift himself. Privately he would have loved to have taken a drink, but never was he going to let her see him again the state she had found him when before, it had all started with him wanting just *one* drink. 'So how did it go today?' he asked.

'Fabulously,' she replied enthusiastically, admitting, 'Though I was a bit ham-fisted with my chopsticks.

And I was terrified the leg I was sitting on was going to go to sleep!'

She then itemised all she had eaten, trying to put some humour into what she was saying. But all too soon she had told him all she could think to tell him, and as his eyes took on the faraway look she was now used to, she blurted out brightly: 'I met Serle Falconer today,' and could not be sorry if she had triggered off more painful memories, since that man was responsible for the mess he was in, when her father left his thoughts to ask when and where had she met him.

'At lunch, or rather just after, Yukiko and I were just putting on our shoes when he and a couple of Japanese men came into the restaurant.'

'He had a couple of Japanese men with him, you say?' queried her father, pleasing her that he had come right away from his despairing thoughts by the look, as with his face showing an interest, he said, 'So that's why a memo went round this morning saying not to interrupt Serle!' How he could still call him Serle defeated her, but she said nothing as he went on, 'He's been working on a project just recently that needs millions pouring into it if it's to get off the ground. And while I'm near certain he's confident enough of his work to put some of his own money in, rumour has been rife this last month that he had a couple of influential bankers interested.' And while Kelsey was already in front of him, he went on, 'I'll bet the two chaps you saw with him were these bankers flown up to have a look at his project.'

As she lay sleepless that night, part of Kelsey thought, serve Falconer right! She hoped he *didn't* get the millions he was after to back his project. That should teach him not to persuade people who couldn't afford it to invest in worthless shares—she hoped he put all *his* money in his pet project, *and* that it all went up the spout.

But against that was the fact that any project that needed millions backing it just had to mean that it kept thousands of people in employment. And remembering the fury in his eyes when in front of what she now knew to be two very financially influential men, she had told him she was particular whom she allowed to shake her hand, and then proceeded to insult him further, she had to see then that it was no small wonder that Serle Falconer had looked as though he had made himself a promise to sort her out at a later date.

Business was invariably discussed over lunch, she knew that. So she guessed that that particular luncheon had been vitally important to him. And she shrank down on her bed then as she saw that any inkling that he was untrustworthy, and he would not stand a chance of his companions passing over so much as a penny of the millions he was after!

Being naturally sensitive, Kelsey took a long time to get to sleep that night. But as she eventually dropped off, it occurred to her to hope, for the sake of those she might have done out of employment, that maybe Falconer's companions hadn't understood English anyway. Though as she surfaced again a few hours later, she had to know that they did, or why else had he been so flaming mad? And, recalling how all three men had laughed heartily, she just had to wonder then, had Serle Falconer added anything else to that bit about her bowing—something which Yukiko had not told her?

Two days later Kelsey had the chance to ask Yukiko that very question. Yukiko had telephoned her just after lunch, and had asked if there was anything particular she would like to do that afternoon. Unsure of how long she would be staying in Japan, and having therefore to be careful with her yen—she had no intention of asking her father for anything from his limited resources—Kelsey said she would like to go for a walk.

As she had given Yukiko some refreshment before

they set off, it was later than they had intended when they started their walk. But it was while they were out, having walked a quarter of a mile to the next village, the mountains in the distance making a breathtakingly beautiful background to the scene, that Kelsey found the ideal moment. Yukiko had paused, causing her to pause with her, beside a large impressive-looking two-storied house where she told her that this was where Falconer-*san* lived.

Trust him to have a bigger house than anyone else around! Kelsey thought sourly, finding in herself vandalistic thoughts she had never possessed in relation to the urge to toss a brick through one of his windows—there had been no rousing her father from the depression he had slumped back into last night.

'Does he own it?' she asked as they walked on.

'I believe he rents it,' replied Yukiko, 'though not from the company, I think.'

'It's a nice house,' said Kelsey, not particularly interested in the dwelling. But, unable to hold back any longer, 'Did Serle Falconer say anything else on Tuesday when we met him—besides that bit about me not shaking hands?'

For a moment Yukiko's face went thoughtful as though she was wondering whether to answer or not. Then suddenly she smiled her warm smile, and replied, 'We were nearly out of the restaurant, but I think I heard him say something about English girls pretending that they do not trust a man purely so that the man will chase after them to get them to change their opinion.'

'*What!*' exclaimed Kelsey, open-mouthed, stunned, at the glib tongue of him, though wondering why she should be, since this was only just so much more evidence of what a smooth talker he was.

'It is not so? I have offended you by repeating this?' questioned Yukiko, seeing she was all but gasping.

About to say that it was very definitely not so, and wishing she had given in to the impulse to throw a brick, or preferably half a dozen, through his windows, Kelsey caught her friend's troubled expression, and since Yukiko would not have said anything if she hadn't prised it out of her, from somewhere she found a smile and settled for:

'Our ways are just a little different from yours, I think.'

An easy companionship having sprung up between them, they forgot the time as they chatted as they walked along, so that by the time they retraced their steps, it was later than either of them had thought.

'Will you come in and say hello to my father?' Kelsey invited, seeing from her father's car parked next to Yukiko's that he had arrived home. But Yukiko was running late, and asked to be excused, and smiling as usual, she got into her car and returned Kelsey's wave.

Having spent a for the most part pleasant afternoon, more pleasant when Serle Falconer was not the subject under discussion, Kelsey entered the small house determined to jolly her father out of his depression that evening. She could tell him about her walk, about the beautiful dragonflies she had seen, about cicadas she had heard but not seen, about . . . Her thoughts broke off as Henry Marchant came along the small hallway to meet her.

'There you are!' he exclaimed, his voice sounding so cheerful, nothing about him of the depressed man she had expected to see, that Kelsey, with joy in her heart, just knew something good had happened for him.

'Sorry I wasn't in when you came home,' she said, holding down the impulse to ask had he heard from her mother as she went with him into the sitting room. For to her mind his cock-a-hoop manner and her mother were synonymous. 'Yukiko and I went for a walk and forgot the time.'

With her father grinning like a Cheshire cat, Kelsey knew he wouldn't be able to hold out for very long before he told her what had happened. And so pleased was she for him that she too was smiling broadly, her heart full to see this change in him from the man he had been, when, as she expected, unable to keep it to himself a minute longer, he said:

'Perhaps it's just as well you were out.' And, that grin emerging again, 'I've had a visitor.'

Knowing full well his visitor could not have been her mother, for he would not so easily let her out of his sight again, Kelsey still thought it must have some connection with her mother. But when he continued, and told her all he had to tell her, the anticipatory smile on her face abruptly vanished.

'A visitor?' she queried, as yet still smiling. 'Who?' she asked—and very nearly dropped, when he chortled:

'A *Nakōdo*.' And while she stared at him un-comprehendingly, knowing the word from somewhere but thinking she must have got her Japanese mixed up, he translated, 'A go-between,' and as her jaw dropped, he added, 'There's been an offer of marriage for you.'

CHAPTER FOUR

'AN offer of *marriage*!' Witlessly, for numbed seconds, Kelsey stared at her parent.

'Well, the initial stages of enquiry, anyway,' Henry Marchant rephrased it. 'A Mr Saito has been engaged as go-between to act between you and—er—the interested party.'

Recovering from her utter astonishment, Kelsey could see that he was tickled pink that a go-between had called. And while she couldn't think of any Japanese man who might want to marry her, for in truth she had barely met any, the indignation that followed her amazement was tempered by the fact that just seeing her father in high spirits after so many evenings of seeing him near to being morose did her heart good. And so it was that wanting him to stay in high spirits, she made no attempt to tell him her views of arranged marriages, but went along with him though only because she was positive that he couldn't be taking the matter seriously either.

'This—er—go-between, this Mr Saito, he called for a photograph of me, did he?' she asked, remembering that this was the way it went.

Her father shaking his head made her realise that this was something she *had* got mixed up. That was until he picked up an envelope that had been reposing unnoticed by her on a small table, and handed it to her, his face serious, though not depressed any longer, she was glad to note.

'Mr Saito's—client has not waited to receive a photograph of you,' he informed her, 'but has sent his own photograph along.'

Kelsey took the envelope he offered, realising

suddenly, and with the first flutterings of unease, that though the idea of someone having her in mind as a marriage partner had restored her father's good humour, he was at heart regarding the matter with every bit as much solemnity as a Japanese.

'Mr Saito will wait to hear from us,' he said, when, her fingers playing along the flap of the envelope, she made no move to open it.

Again it was being endorsed for her that her father was not treating the matter as lightly as she had at first thought. For surely, had he considered the go-between's business at their home lightly, he would not have let him leave the photograph behind when he went!

Having her answer ready before she saw which Japanese man was showing an interest in her, Kelsey took her eyes from her parent as she pulled back the flap of the envelope. Then with the snapshot in her fingers, not a studio portrait as she would have thought, still in no hurry, she pulled the small photo from its wrapping.—And exploded with anger!

The swine, she thought, *that* swine! For the photograph of the man who looked back at her, taken by the use of some automatic release, if she wasn't mistaken; a photograph taken that way because he either was contemptuous of portrait studios, or did not care to have anyone take his photograph, was none other than that of the man she hated above all others.

'Serle must have taken a big fancy to you when he saw you the other day,' said Henry Marchant when, keeping her head bent, she stared disbelievingly at the snapshot in her hand. But at his tone, not amused in any way, Kelsey lifted her angry head.

My God, she thought, he *is* taking this seriously! His voice had conveyed that much without that look on his face that said he was fully prepared to go along with the idea.

'I . . .' she choked, but was speechless. And needing time, for some sixth sense told her that if she said any of what was in her mind his depression would descend like some dark overhanging cloud, she again turned her attention to the picture in her hand.

The swine, was all she could think, as ignoring the fact that Serle Falconer was not all that bad looking, she espied only that that was a definite smirk he had on his face as he'd waited for his camera to click. Damn you, Falconer, she fumed silently as it came to her that she had not been mistaken when she had read a murderous-looking threat in his eyes after she had insulted him. He had meant then, to get even with her—and this was his way of doing it. That look on his face said it all. That 'I'll teach you to mess with me' look.

But there was no time then for her to delve any deeper into the whys and the wherefores of Serle Falconer doing what he had. Time only to be aware that knowing as he did exactly how she viewed arranged marriages, he had sent along a go-between together with his photograph, as though to say, 'Now get out of that!'

Puzzled that he should think for one moment that she couldn't 'Get out of that', Kelsey raised her head again as her father enquired, to her alarm in all sincerity, 'Well—what do you think?'

No, no, no, I'd rather die, said her head, 'Er—he looks more than able to find a wife for himself—without needing to employ—a go-between,' she muttered from that sensitivity in her that had feared a breakdown in her beloved parent, who now, however, looked to have come a long way from the man he had been last evening.

'He must want to marry an English girl,' her father replied, offering for an explanation, 'They aren't very thick on the ground around here.'

'But if he wants to marry an English girl, why adopt a Japanese method to do his—er—courting?' she asked, trying without actually having to say so to get him to see that there was no way this little charade was going any further.

'Serle's a very busy man,' he answered, with none of the malice she had hoped to hear against the man who had so treacherously been the ultimate cause of his ruin. Which thought had her heart hardening further against Serle Falconer, and softening to putty for her father, that the goodness in him bore that dreadful man no ill will. 'And what with this project he's been working so hard on looking like coming to fruition, it must mean that he intends to stay in Japan longer than was first thought. With him sending Mr Saito here today,' he expanded, 'it must mean that he intends to settle in Japan—that he wants to settle and marry. And since he probably thinks your holiday will end soon, he's had to move this way or lose all chance with you.'

That Serle Falconer didn't have *any* chance with her, nor, as she knew full well, did he want one, touched only fleetingly down just then. For, something in what her father said about that loathsome man intending to settle in Japan made her thoughts bolt to the staggering possibility of—could it be that her father had no objection to raise because, loving her mother so much; knowing her expressed desire to see more of her daughter, his vision was clouded by the overwhelming hope that if she settled in Japan too, then his wife, longing to be near her, would return to Japan for that very purpose!

'So what do you think, Kelsey?' he asked, his voice earnest now as he waited for her answer.

Kelsey made the mistake of looking at him. She realised that too late when, instead of him killing the idea stone dead before it went any further, she looked up and the pleading in his eyes got to her; his eyes just seemed to be begging her not to dismiss the idea out of hand.

'I—I . . .' she found herself stammering. And as she saw him swallow on some emotion, weakly, she heard herself say, 'I'll—think about it, Dad.'

Henry Marchant's depression did not return that night—he had handed it on to his daughter. And alone in her room Kelsey just sat and stared into space as her mind tried to cope with the boggle of complications that had been growing in her ever since she had returned from her walk with Yukiko. For the longer she spent with her parent that evening, the more it had become clearer and clearer that he had indeed spent so long in Japan that not only did he seem to be able to accept their customs, but that he saw nothing at all wrong in those customs being applied to his daughter too.

Of a certainty he did not feel it as incredible as she did to accept that a man she barely knew—as far as he knew their only acquaintanceship had been that of bumping into each other in a restaurant—should make overtures of marriage for her. Though of course he must have seen enough go-between arranged marriages in his time here for it not to appear anything out of the ordinary, but—even for his own daughter!

Having time she hadn't had before to look into the whole of it, Kelsey found that she didn't quite believe in her theory that his vision was clouded by the hope that his wife would return to Japan if she settled there. And she was on then to thinking of the money he owed—lost money he didn't want his Eve to know about!

Oh dear, she sighed, as a fresh and unwanted thought tumbled into her head. A thought she didn't want, a thought she regarded as so disloyal she didn't want to face it. Yet it was a thought that had to be faced as she checked back; was it only that her father was now so orientated to the Japanese way of life that he couldn't see anything wrong in Serle Falconer sending Mr Saito to call? Was it only that he thought her mother would come to Japan if she settled there—aside from having to explain about the smaller house and other issues, a long shot, surely, even if he was in a cleft stick situation and ready to grab at any straw? Or was it neither of the two?

Having to face it, much as she didn't want to, Kelsey fell to wondering about the third and, hating herself for her thoughts, the most likely possibility—was it that her father, a near to broken man to her way of thinking, believed that with the wealthy Serle Falconer for a son-in-law all his money problems would be over?

Hating herself even as she made herself finish the thought through to the end, Kelsey stifled a groan her father might have heard through the thin walls, as it came to her that this last explanation for his jubilation when she had returned from her walk fitted far better than the other two.

But, disgusted as she was for allowing such disloyal thoughts, she again saw that smirk on Serle Falconer's face in the snapshot he had sent. And all at once she knew that he had thought it all out too, damn him, and that he too had come to the same conclusions that she had.

The swine, she thought for the umpteenth time. The diabolical, devilish, damnable swine! He knew perfectly well she'd commit hara-kiri before she would consider marrying him! But by approaching her father first, he knew too, since he had positive proof how much she loved her parent from the way she had gone for Serle in his office, that she couldn't pass the message back to him to 'Go to hell' because he too must have seen, and must be aware, as she had told him, that her father was but a shadow of his former self. And, the swine, she thought again, acting on impulse and getting his picture from her bag and tearing it to pieces, he just damn well knew that her father would be pleased to welcome him and his finances into their family!

The overbearing, over-confident pig! she fumed, it wasn't her father who was in a cleft stick—it was her! Serle Falconer knew her father was broke—she had imparted that piece of knowledge herself.

She remembered the 'Now get out of that' expression on Serle Falconer's face, and she knew he had only done it to make her squirm and wriggle. He knew damn well she wouldn't go along with it, she fumed. And she was hating him with all that was in her as she suddenly saw just how much squirming and wriggling she would have to do. Because if she told her father straight out to tell Falconer to 'Get lost', that would have him losing all hope and, depressed again, heading nearer and nearer towards that breakdown.

Swine! she thought furiously. Even if in all probability he did not see her father daily as she did, he couldn't be aware of just how down he was. Serle Falconer certainly wanted his full revenge for her insulting him in front of his influential business acquaintances, didn't he?

When Kelsey at last managed to fall asleep, it was to dream of blue eyes gone dark with threat and menace. And waking from a nightmarish dream where Serle Falconer was towering over her and telling her, 'You tangled with the wrong man when you tangled with me, girl,' she got out of her bed at dawn, and did not feel like returning to it.

'You're up early,' said Henry Marchant, coming into the kitchen, a look of enquiry on his face as though he was asking if she had come to any decision yet.

Alone in the kitchen, nothing seeming quite as terrible in the light of day as it had seemed last night, Kelsey had thought she was ready to give her father the message for Serle Falconer she dearly wanted to. But face to face with him, seeing the anxiety back in his eyes, she could not say, 'Tell Falconer to take a running jump!'

Unable to give him the message she wanted to, just as she was unable to dash her father's hopes, she settled for letting him believe that she hadn't lain awake thinking through half the night. 'I have a lot to think about today,' she said brightly, letting him believe she was making an early start.

But as he left for his office, she found that she was indeed thinking again, and on the same theme. Perhaps

Serle Falconer making out she was preferring to act like a Japanese with her bow had put the idea into his head, she found herself thinking. Perhaps that, on top of her saying that she would never consider an arranged marriage, had triggered off this way to get back at her. But he knew perfectly well that she would not so much as contemplate marrying anyone this way, she fumed, that of course being precisely why he had chosen this mode of revenge. Not only had he put her in a position he knew would make her sweat while trying to wriggle out from, but he had also meant to give her the shock of her life.

That he didn't want to marry her either was beside the point. He ... Her thoughts stopped dead right there. And suddenly an angelic smile began curving her mouth as she backtracked and dwelt on the absolutely gorgeous idea that had started with that unquestionable truth—Serle didn't want to marry her either!

Oh, it was just too too beautiful. Kelsey was almost purring as she thought the idea through. Falconer had started this—let *him* be the one to finish it! And he would, went her thoughts. He'd be calling it off so fast, the go-between would be at the little bungalow again in double quick time!

Five minutes later, thankful that the home where her father used to live still had the same telephone number, because she would never have found it in the Japanese phone book, Kelsey dialled.

Almost at once the phone was picked up. *'Moshi moshi,'* she heard, and was relieved to recognise Yukiko's voice, for had someone who did not speak English answered, Kelsey knew her call would have been fruitless.

'It's Kelsey here,' she told her friend. And in the next breath she was rushing in with her request and was realising what a true friend Yukiko was turning out to be, in that she did not question, but on hearing that Kelsey's need was immediate, replied:

'I will be with you inside the half hour, and will bring the things you wish to borrow with me.'

Two hours later, Yukiko stood back to view her handiwork. 'I think I have got it as nearly right as possible,' she said, studying the calendar portrait which Kelsey had filched from the kitchen wall which showed a Japanese girl complete with kimono, black shining wig, and a painted face. Yukiko then looked at Kelsey. 'Yes,' she said, nodding as she considered her, 'you look exactly like a Japanese girl. Do you wish to see?'

Sitting on the *tatami* of her bedroom floor, Kelsey, her back to her bedroom mirror, took the hand mirror the other girl handed over for her to have a closer inspection. And as she looked at her white-painted face, the thin black eyebrows Yukiko had painted in, and the small red Cupid's bow Yukiko had made of her mouth, all topped with a black wig that covered her fair hair, so the corners of the rest of Kelsey's mouth curved upwards.

'It's fabulous—absolutely fabulous!' she crowed with delight. 'Thank you so much, Yukiko.'

'My pleasure,' replied Yukiko. Then, seeming to hesitate, 'But do you really wish me to take your photograph looking like that?' And explaining again just in case Kelsey had not understood her English the first time, 'It is not usual for a Japanese girl to have her portrait taken for such an occasion with the white-painted face.'

Kelsey had had to tell Yukiko, though swearing her to secrecy, something, though not all, of what was going on. And on hearing that Mr Falconer had sent a go-between to see her father, Yukiko had beamed happily for all the world as though, while not understanding Kelsey's ploy in the restaurant when she had pretended she did not want to know him, it had after all worked out the way, according to Falconer-*san*, it was supposed to work.

'Mr Falconer had chosen the Japanese way by

approaching me through my father,' Kelsey replied, not wanting to deceive her, but since she was unable to tell her the full truth, having to go along with what she had started. 'But I think he will understand that I must paint my face to let him know that I am not fully conversant with the way things are done.'

Appearing to be on the point of telling her that she would willingly instruct her, Yukiko changed her mind as though thinking perhaps the English girl would prefer it this way. 'If you arc ready, then, Kelsey-*san*,' she said.

And while Kelsey posed, and thought mutinously, 'Now *you* get out of that, Mr Serle Falconer!' for surely he was going to die of a heart attack when he received her photograph and the message that would go with it—the last thing he was expecting was that she would take him up on it—Yukiko got busy with her polaroid.

A minute later Kelsey was staring at the picture Yukiko had just taken. Staring back at her was the most demure-looking face, Japanese down to the last detail—that was until one looked at the eyes. Oh, my word, Kelsey thought, supremely satisfied. She might verbally be sending the message that she was prepared to accept him as a suitor, but—she barely remembered what she had been thinking of when the camera Yukiko had brought with her had clicked—but as sure as eggs, those eyes were very definitely sending the message, 'You can go to hell!'

'Is it all right? Shall I take another?' queried Yukiko doubtfully when Kelsey had studied the picture at some length.

'This one's fine, just fine,' Kelsey replied, never more rewarded. 'But I really must get out of your costume— I'm roasting alive!'

Once out of the kimono, the decorative *obi* removed from around her middle, Kelsey lost no time in rinsing the make-up from her face.

They celebrated their labours with a well earned cup

of coffee. But when she asked Yukiko if she knew where Mr Saito lived, and told her that she intended taking her photograph to his house, Yukiko would not hear of it.

'It is not right,' she said firmly. 'But if you are desirous of him having your picture straight away,' she smiled, as if suddenly realising how eager her friend was that she couldn't wait for her father to begin negotiations, 'then I will take it to Mr Saito for you.'

Of the opinion that Yukiko had done more than enough for her, even if the Japanese girl had expressed her delight to help, Kelsey would have argued. But when she told her that Mr Saito lived three miles distant, and that she had to go near his house on her way home, the half mile or so out of her way being neither here nor there in her car, plus the fact that there was every chance that he did not speak English, Kelsey had to give in.

'But you will be sure that he understands that I'm willing?' Kelsey asked her.

'Be easy in your mind,' replied the other, 'I shall not fail you, Kelsey-*san*.'

After Yukiko had gone, Kelsey went to her room to look at the kimono she had left behind. With typical kindness, Yukiko had wanted to give her the pretty kimono, and had left it in case she should change her mind about accepting it. I'll give it back to her when I tell her that Falconer has withdrawn his suit, she thought. And she went to rinse through the coffee cups and saucers they had used, her mind given over to a mixture of thoughts.

She would have to try and make it up to her father somehow, she thought. For, from the cheerful way he had been last night, he was going to be sorely disappointed that the next visit from the go-between would be to tell him that Serle Falconer had changed his mind.

Her elation on seeing the picture of herself looking,

apart from her eyes, like some demure Japanese maiden *with* pretty manners was far from her later that afternoon when she pondered, was she being cowardly to let Falconer do the dirty work?

But later still, having defended her action by thinking he had only done it anyway to make her squirm, she didn't think she was being cowardly at all. Let him do his own dirty work—why should she do it for him? Perhaps then her father, who already had ample proof of how worthless his word was, would start calling him Falconer too, the way she did.

A feeling of satisfaction came to her again as she visualised Falconer's face when Mr Saito told him that the lady was willing. She'd like to bet he would drop dead with the shock of it!

Kelsey's head was still full of Serle Falconer; not normally a vindictive person, she was having happy thoughts of letting him do some squirming for a change, when her father's arrival home put all thoughts of anyone save him and his disappointment from her mind.

As yesterday, he greeted her looking as if he had said goodbye to the depression that had had such a grip on him that he had not been able to shake it off even for her.

'Had a good day?' she asked. But although he answered her without that bleak look in his eyes, she didn't miss that question they held that asked, 'Have you come to a decision yet?'

Over their meal they chatted about everything under the sun but her mother and Serle Falconer. Though it had to be said that once or twice, compunction gripping her, Kelsey very nearly came right out with it and told him herself that Falconer wasn't serious, rather than let him wait until tomorrow—the earliest, she thought, that Falconer would send back word.

But, as the evening progressed, the more and more she thought about it, the more Kelsey grew of the opinion that with her father, after being led up the garden path about those shares, still looking up to Falconer, then perhaps when not losing his respect for the man for what he had done to him, might, when a member of his own family was taken for a ride through his worthless word, then find very little to respect in the man, and might then see him in his true colours.

They were both surprised when just after nine that evening the door bell announced that they had a visitor. 'Who . . .!' Henry Marchant started to exclaim, getting to his feet, for not once during Kelsey's stay had anyone called this late.

Kelsey had another surprise when her father came back into the sitting room, bringing a man in with him whom he introduced as Mr Saito, explaining, as Yukiko had suggested might be the case, that Mr Saito spoke only Japanese.

'*Konbahnwa,*' she offered her 'Good evening' in reply to his formal greeting, her eyes shooting to her father, knowing what the go-between's call was all about as Henry Marchant turned from him to translate that Mr Saito was apologising for the lateness of his visit, but that he had called on his client a short while ago, and it had been impressed upon him that he must come to their home without delay.

I'll bet it was, Kelsey thought. But she couldn't help a feeling of surprise that her 'I'm willing' reply had so panicked Falconer that he had sent the go-between to terminate his business tonight. Somehow she hadn't thought of Falconer being the panicky sort; even if she had frightened the life out of him with the shape of her answer.

But her triumph that she had Falconer running scared was shortlived, quashed by the sobering dilemma of—should she stay and help her father when depression fell on him as he heard what the go-between had come to say—all hope gone of him being reunited with his Eve—or should she courteously leave the two men alone together?

One glance at her father and she saw that he was determined that their guest should be accorded all the respect his position in these negotiations demanded. And she saw then that he had enough pride not to let Mr Saito know the devastating blow he had delivered. Politely she excused herself and left the room.

But in her bedroom, Serle Falconer no longer figuring in her thoughts, she was on thorns while making herself stay put. She was unable to make out anything from the conversation she could hear through the thin walls, but when after ten tormented minutes had passed she heard the clink of glasses, she guessed that her father was keeping up a front and offering Mr Saito some refreshment.

Hoping that he would stick to just the one drink and not try to drown his sorrows when their visitor had left, when another ten minutes had passed and Mr Saito was still there, she had come round to the view that it had been self-indulgent of her to want to do Serle Falconer one in the eye. Fair enough, he needed his come-uppance, but it would have been better for her father if she had told him herself.

When at last she did hear movement that indicated Mr Saito was on his way, Kelsey was near to hating herself for what had that morning seemed a perfect way to turn the tables on Falconer and make him be the one to wriggle.

She waited then only to hear her parent come back from seeing Mr Saito to the door, and she was meeting him in the hall. Though to her surprise, she heard him ask:

'Well, young lady, what's this I hear you've been up to?'

She was surprised again as, preceding him into the sitting room, she saw that he was back again to covering up his feelings. Solemnly she faced him, seeing exactly what a brave act he was putting on. For there was absolutely nothing about him to show how down he was really feeling, when he said:

'I reckon you must have been as smitten with Serle at that first meeting as he was with you—only you were too shy to tell your old dad that you were willing.'

Kelsey felt the first faint pricklings of alarm that, while knowing from Mr Saito that she had sent word she was willing, he was smiling. He should definitely not be smiling, she thought, not now he had the returned-with-all-speed message from Serle Falconer that unfortunately he had gone off the idea.

'Er—Yukiko went and saw Mr Saito for me,' she owned.

'So I've been told,' he replied. And waggishly, sending another dart of alarm through her, 'If we're going to do this the Japanese way, you're going to have to leave more to me, child.'

Kelsey didn't like at all the words 'going to'. To her mind it sounded very much as though her father imagined there were 'going to' be future negotiations. Not speaking any but the most basic of basic Japanese herself, she had to pause then to wonder how good her father's fluent Japanese was. Surely he had got it wrong, for he was going on while she was batting off fresh spears of alarm, and telling her:

'Serle really must be keen, that he didn't want to wait until tomorrow for Mr Saito to call on his behalf.'

That word 'keen' was another one she didn't like, and had a whole barrowload of spears sending their shafts of panic through her. Panic she tried to control because she knew full well she had given Falconer something to panic over and not the other way around.

'I expect he wanted to let you know before . . .' She couldn't get the 'before you started to bank on it' out.

'Before tomorrow, so we don't make alternative arrangements for the evening,' her father took up and finished for her.

'Alternative arrangement!' Kelsey exclaimed, confusion and panic mingling. 'Arrangements for what?'

If Henry Marchant noticed that she was staring at him wide eyed and looked a little pale in her bewilderment, then he was easily able to put it down to her lack of knowledge of Japanese customs.

'Why, for the family meeting, of course,' he replied, enlightening her further by telling her that it was usual, when all parties were agreed, for the parents of the man and the parents of the girl all to meet, together with their offspring, at some public place. 'Of course Serle's parents aren't in Japan,' and, his face sobering for a moment, 'and your mother can't be at the meeting either,' and brighter again, 'so that leaves you, me and Serle.'

Very near to choking as she tried to get her words out, all Kelsey, in a numbed state of shock, was able to utter was, 'You mean that—you and—and I—and . . .'

'And Serle,' said her father, having no trouble with the name that wouldn't pass her lips, 'are dining together tomorrow night.'

'B-but . . .' was as far as her protest could get. It was all wrong. Her father must have got it wrong. There must be some error through his not being so fluent in the language as she had thought he was. 'B-but . . .' she stammered again.

'I know,' he said, on a teasing tone, 'you've got nothing to wear.' Then, 'Don't worry about it, love. Serle saw you once when you hadn't dressed up specially for him. It's you with your sweet ways he wants to see tomorrow night, not what you're wearing.'

Sweet ways! Kelsey thought when, still shattered, she bade her father goodnight, having heard from him the name of the restaurant where Falconer had told Mr Saito they were to meet him—which meant, since he had named a meeting place, that there had been no error in language. Heavens she thought, if Falconer could read in her mind half the far from sweet things she was wishing him, he'd be regretting having picked up the gauntlet she had been unconscious of throwing down!

How long she lay there fuming impotently against Serle Falconer, Kelsey had no idea. But to start with she had been of the opinion that he would have a very long wait if he intended her to turn up at that restaurant tomorrow night.

But, independent-minded as she was, angry as she always was when she thought of him, this last episode topping the lot as far as she was concerned, there was that something in her that just totally rebelled against being the first to back down.

That rebellion was as strong as ever when she awakened the next morning and her eyes caught sight of Yukiko's kimono hanging on the top of the screen door. Kelsey knew then, as her anger against Serle Falconer went soaring, that she was just not going to be the first to back down.

So Falconer had come courting Japanese style, had he! Well, so be it. Her father thought her hesitancy last night had sprung from her having nothing to wear, but, as her eyes went again to the kimono, Kelsey thought she had the very thing. If she had got it right, and she was sure she had, the intended bride traditionally always wore a kimono at that first formal meeting. So if she knew it, Falconer must know it too, and since he had probably chosen a restaurant where he was well known, then everyone else in the restaurant would know too, when she turned up in Yukiko's kimono, that Falconer wanted to marry her.

Beautiful wasn't the word for it, she thought, a contented smile tracing her mouth. Falconer hadn't managed to remain a bachelor at his age without putting in some nifty leg work, he'd soon be backing down—why, it wouldn't surprise her in the least if he started his sprint from the moment he saw her!

CHAPTER FIVE

KELSEY was putting the finishing touches to her costume that evening when she heard her father's enquiry of 'Ready, Kelsey?' through the partitioning of her bedroom. 'We're going to be late!'

Good, she thought, but called back, 'I'll be only a minute.'

Taking a look at herself in the mirror that stood in the corner, she was pleased with her appearance save that Yukiko had taken her black wig with her when she had gone yesterday, and her own fair, blonde-streaked hair was waving down about her shoulders. She'd had to settle for her normal light make-up too, when she would liked to have given Falconer something more to think about by wearing the same make-up she had worn for her photograph. Though she was doubtful if the white make-up was traditional for this particular occasion, and anyway she didn't have Yukiko's artistry. Apart from which, he was good at laughing at her, was Falconer, without the need for her to turn up looking like a clown to give him more fuel for his perverted sense of humour.

With the wooden *geta* on her feet that Yukiko had also left behind, a must, in Kelsey's view, with the kimono, she left her room to go in search of her father, thinking that provided she didn't try to go rushing about anywhere in the wooden clogs, she should not come to any grief. But then she wasn't rushing anywhere tonight—let Falconer wait!

'Serle will think we're not com . . .' Her father broke off his complaint as she joined him and his eyes caught sight of the way she was dressed. 'Good heavens, child,' he exclaimed, looking at her in disbelief, 'you can't go out in that thing, everyone will laugh at you!'

As long as they laughed at Falconer too, Kelsey, as angry as ever when she thought of that man, didn't care one tiny bit.

'Don't be stuffy, Dad,' she said, forcing a smile. 'Anything goes these days.' And, pretending to be worried at his opinion that she would be laughed at, 'I can go and change if you like, but it will mean getting the iron out—though it shouldn't take me too l . . .'

'Oh, come on,' he said, a stickler for punctuality. 'We're going to be late as it is.'

Perhaps Falconer will have grown tired of waiting, she thought hopefully. Perhaps he had never intended to be there to start with, she wondered, but had sent the go-between with his message just for the sheer hell of it.

She was in no hurry to leave the car when, having found a parking space, Henry Marchant hurried to get them moving. Then suddenly he was taking time out from rushing her along to look at her, his affection for her showing as he quietly, as if he suspected she was having last-minute nerves and that his remark about everyone laughing at her hadn't helped, squeezed her hand and told her:

'You've inherited your mother's beauty, Kelsey love.' And, 'That outfit suits you.'

Feeling choked, because she had never felt this close to him, she sought round and found a bright smile, mumbling, 'I did want to look my best tonight.'

With slow progress lest she missed her footing in her *geta* and went sprawling, eventually they reached the restaurant where they were to meet Serle Falconer, and Henry Marchant stepped back to allow her to enter first.

But Kelsey was keeping her eyes low, hoping to look demure and not at all as inwardly boiling against Falconer as she felt. And it was Henry Marchant who spotted that not only had their host turned up, but that he was still in fact waiting for them.

Kelsey felt her father's hand come firmly to her elbow in case she was all of a twitter inside with nerves, and as she tripped daintily beside him, he escorted her to where Serle Falconer had risen to welcome them.

'My apologies for keeping you waiting, Serle,' said Henry, far too affable with the villain, to Kelsey's way of thinking, 'but Kelsey wanted to look her best tonight.'

Wishing she hadn't told him that bit, she just had to raise her eyes to see if he was yet on his starting blocks. Abruptly she lowered them. The swine, she thought, she was the one who felt like running at seeing nothing in his eyes save a glimmer of amusement that said he was far from put out, all that glorious anticipation of hers so much pie in the sky.

'Your daughter is well worth waiting for, Henry,' she heard him say smoothly.

Anger pricked her, making her not want to run anywhere. You toad! she fumed uselessly, mutiny she couldn't hope to hide flashing as she again looked at him.

Brown eyes clashed with blue. His expression bland, although she guessed he was reading in hers that it would give her the greatest pleasure to take another swipe at him.

'How are you, Kelsey?' he enquired with some charm.

My God, he's risking it! she thought, when accompanying his enquiry, just as though he didn't remember that at their last meeting she had refused to shake hands with him, he stretched out his hand to her.

To find that her own hand was coming out to meet his, when it had not been her intention to shake hands with him, must, she thought, be the result of Gran instilling in her the importance of good manners. That and the fact that her father was there and could be made to feel uncomfortable if she ignored that outstretched hand as she wanted to. It was not, she definitely decided, because of the glint that had come to Serle Falconer's eyes when he saw that she had hesitated.

She felt his hand close on hers. But when, after brief contact, she decided she had gone far enough to comply with good manners, and went to withdraw her hand, Kelsey found that extra pressure was being applied, that extra pressure being applied to pull her up close. And that far from being put out that she had appeared in her 'let everybody know what this meeting was about' kimono, Serle Falconer was taking it on himself to remove all formality out of their handshake, making them look less than strangers, by placing cool firm lips against her cheek.

Had she been more certain of her footing, Kelsey was certain she would have aimed a kick at his shin. As it was, instinct made her push him away, but only to hear him murmur before he let go of her:

'Your picture didn't do you justice.'

Why she should colour at his remark, she didn't know. But her colour was still high as she took her seat in the Western-style furnished restaurant.

From the fond look her father sent her, she knew he had noted her heightened colour and was putting it down to a shyness in her that Falconer had publicly demonstrated that his interest in her went further than that of hand-shaking friends. Then he was launching without more ado into conversation with Serle Falconer—his way, she guessed, of giving her a few moments to get over her shyness.

But she was glad of a few minutes to collect her thoughts. Swine! she thought again; she had been so sure Falconer would fall apart to see her dressed as she was—that he should be amused was untenable. She wasn't feeling very friendly towards her father either, that he seemed to think the kiss Serle Falconer had bestowed on her cheek was only right and natural in the circumstances.

Creep, she thought, when Falconer gravely asked her if she had any preference as to what she would like to eat. No doubt in her mind he had chosen the Western-style restaurant in deference to her father who, for all he was a fit man, might suffer the same near dead leg she had experienced when eating from one of the low tables. After what he had done they didn't want or need his small courtesies.

The menu meant nothing to her, though it was a help to see that there was a photograph of each of the meals listed showing them as they would appear at the table.

'Might I suggest *sukiyaki*, Kelsey?' She looked at Falconer, who in order to help her with her choice had moved his chair that little bit closer to hers. She'd be damned if she'd eat *sukiyaki* or anything else he suggested!

'We could all have *sukiyaki*,' her father came in, without knowing it tempering her aggression and making her wonder if her antipathy to Serle Falconer had caused her to be small-minded. 'Not much point in them setting up a hotplate just for one,' he added reasonably.

Sukiyaki when it arrived turned out to be various bowls of vegetables and thinly sliced beef which one cooked oneself over the heated hotplate plugged into a socket by their table.

She blamed it on to her kimono that whereas the two men, both adept with chopsticks, she didn't doubt, were offered the choice of a knife and fork, that offer was not made to her. And with both of them saying that chopsticks would be fine, it was beneath her to request a knife and fork for herself.

Consequently, while Henry Marchant and Serle Falconer tucked in as though eating was going out of style, Kelsey, limiting herself to only the pieces she thought she could pick up without dropping them all over Yukiko's kimono, ate very little—and once very nearly came to grief with a piece of mushroom she had selected that turned out to be very wayward, and slipped back from whence she had got it.

'This piece, Kelsey?' said the silky-voiced Falconer, who had been the soul of courtesy and charm throughout the meal.

'Thank you,' she muttered, her words reaching the other two even to her own ears sounding totally devoid of any of the polite charm Serle Falconer had been sending her way. It was her father's sharp look that made her dredge up a smile, for him that she pushed Falconer's first name out through her teeth. 'Serle,' she added, then concentrated on the mushroom he had expertly deposited into her dish.

By the time the meal came to an end, she was, but very definitely, out of sorts. For one thing, wearing the kimono had been a mistake. Apart from her not being Japanese, and feeling totally unlike the way she thought a Japanese girl would feel on such an occasion, she was finding that the kimono and all its accessories made her feel very hot and uncomfortable. And for another thing, her father was treating Serle Falconer much too kindly, in her view. Why, it was almost as if, while having concrete evidence of how unreliable his word was, he was treating every word Falconer uttered as gospel.

Of course, it could be that her father was play-acting the same way that she was; that wanting her to marry Falconer he was putting to the back of his mind what he really thought of him. Against that, though, was the knowledge that her father wasn't really like that— though, unhappily Kelsey had to face it, her mother leaving him had shown tendencies in his character she would never have attributed to him. Never would she have thought to see him so drunk that he could hardly stand. Never had she ever thought to see him in tears. And, remembering the laughing-eyed man he had always been, never would she have thought him to be so depressed that he was next door to a breakdown.

And there was evidence, too, that he was exhausted. Because although it was still fairly early, and he was a man with energy to spare, she had always thought, suddenly, barely finishing his green tea, he was putting down his cup and declaring:

'I'm feeling just a little tired.' Her concerned eyes shot to him, but he was looking not at her but at their host as he said, 'Would you mind if I called it a day?'

Serle Falconer had risen and had murmured a bland, 'Not at all,' when Kelsey went to get to her feet to go with her father. The hand that came to her shoulder held her down. 'I'll see Kelsey home,' he added, that phoney charm in evidence again.

Like hell you will! she thought, but found she was going nowhere as that grip on her shoulder refused to let her up, as bending his head to her ear, Falconer breathed, 'Do, Kelsey, allow your father to be tactful, there's a dear.'

Tactful! That she had contributed little to the conversation she didn't doubt was being put down by her father to the shyness he thought he had seen in her. But as Serle Falconer refused to let go his hold on her, only then did she see that 'tactful' was what her parent thought he was being by professing tiredness.

He thought she wanted to be left alone with the wretched man! Almost too late, as she gave another ineffectual tug to get free from the softly smiling man who was instructing her father to drive carefully, did she realise she could ruin it all now if she wasn't careful. It had to be Falconer who was the first to back down. That admission to her father that there was never likely to be anything between the two of them had to come from him.

'I'll—see you later, Dad,' she said, when he eventually seemed to notice that Serle Falconer appeared to have a very protective hand on her shoulder.

Henry Marchant smiled. Then, 'Don't be too late,' he said, as if seeing that protective hand had reminded him that he had a duty to be protective too.

The moment he was out of sight and not likely to turn round and witness her action, Kelsey shrugged off Serle Falconer's hold. That he allowed to let her go was, she knew, because there seemed small likelihood of her chasing after the man who had just left.

Thinking to give her father time only to get clear before she took herself off in a taxi—the rat Falconer was driving her nowhere!—she watched as he resumed his seat, but inwardly seething. She had nothing she wanted to say to him.

Though when she had counted three minutes, intending to give her father five, and Falconer hadn't spoken either, she was annoyed with herself to find she was wondering what it was he was thinking. She annoyed herself further when, suspecting he had his eyes on the decor, or anywhere but her, she could not refrain from taking a flicker of a glance at him.

He was not looking about or at the décor, but was, contrary to her surmise, looking at no one but her. And he seemed, although the charm and surface politeness he had shown while her father was there had gone, to have been studying her for some while!

Kelsey had had enough. She cared little more for his detached scrutiny, for the cool lofty mocking indifference in the way he looked back at her—just as if he was in charge of everything—than she cared for him.

Without saying a word, she rose from the table, making sure the *geta* on her feet were correctly positioned before she made her daintily footstepped way across the restaurant floor.

Halfway to the door, she halted and turned to face the man who she hadn't missed had risen too, and who had been right behind her. There was something she had to make very clear—and right now!

'Courtesy compels me to thank you for my dinner,' she offered coldly. 'But a lift home with you I just *don't need*.'

Her words were greeted with a slightly scandalised look that, together with the words he drawled, made her long to hammer the living daylights out of him.

'Would I allow my near-fiancée to travel home unescorted? What an opinion you must have of me, my dear!'

She very nearly thumped him then, and knew not from where she got sufficient self-control to keep her hands to herself at his words 'near-fiancée' let alone the 'my dear'. And as for her opinion of him, once she got started on that, it would be midnight before she was finished!

'I,' she said clearly, 'am going home in a taxi.' And when he shook his head slowly from side to side in contradiction, her anger broke, and she was hissing at him, 'I am not your near-fiancée, Falconer, nor ever am I likely to be!' And when he stopped shaking his head and looked likely to nod it again in contradiction, this time Kelsey forgot that there were other diners in earshot, and stopped hissing to say loudly, forcefully, 'The joke is over!'

His reply, the words that came with not a flicker of an eyelid from him, the cool, 'Who's joking?' had her very near to clobbering him right there.

Only just did she recover sufficient awareness of her whereabouts not to hit him with some force. Instead, she took one deep and furious breath and turned about, damning her footwear as well as him that she couldn't break into a gallop the sooner to be shot of him. She knew positively—*him* with his 'Who's joking?'—that he'd start foaming at the mouth if he thought she was playing this for real!

Of course it had to be her luck that there wasn't a

sign of a taxi in the vicinity. And when it had been him she had wanted to embarrass, as she observed several passers-by giving her curious looks as she stood looking up and down the street in her borrowed kimono, one lady actually breaking out into a giggle as she passed, it was Kelsey who was left feeling embarrassed.

Her face went pink as no taxi appeared and more curious glances were directed her way, her hate for Falconer reaching a peak that he was propped up against a wall not twenty yards from her, his hands idly in his pockets as he witnessed her discomfiture with what she could only think was pleasure.

There was a smile on his face anyway, when bored with the scene, he at last came over to where she was standing. And that firm hand was under her elbow this time, as with the know-it-all words, 'Taxis never come down this street,' he turned her.

If she had known her way back to her father's house, Kelsey was certain that even with the *geta* she had on, she would have attempted to walk it. But to get lost, probably with Falconer right behind her to witness her further humiliation, was not to be thought of.

His car was sleek and smooth, like she knew it would be—like him, she thought. Though she had to own some relief to be inside and away from gently curious and, she remembered, amused eyes.

But though she did not know in which direction she lived, as Serle Falconer directed his car away from the congestion of traffic and into the rural area, all of a sudden, not seeing any landmarks she recognised, Kelsey began to wonder where he was taking her—or if indeed he was taking her to her father's home. Stubbornly, though, she wouldn't ask him. The only word she wanted to say to him was goodbye.

But she almost broke her silence when the speed of the car slowed. It took her aback, though why it should she couldn't think, but when the car slowed down to a crawl and then halted in the side of a country road, she felt most oddly let down. Somehow, though she had never consciously thought about it, she hadn't considered Falconer to be a lay-by stop-and-grab sort of merchant.

She still hadn't got her voice when she felt him move in his seat and turn towards her as he crooked his arm along the back of his seat.

'Who goes first, you or me?' she heard him ask in the darkness, his features outlined in what light there was of the night.

'What?' she asked, startled. This type of opening gambit was one she hadn't heard before.

'Henry left the two of us alone so we could get to know each other better,' he explained, sounding so very serious that for one crazy moment she felt panic. Panic that started to get out of hand as she remembered his 'Who's joking?' when she had told him that the joke had gone far enough. My God, he *can't* be as serious as he sounds! she thought. Then her panic was harnessed as she remembered that murderous threat in his eyes that day she had insulted him. She knew then that he was playing it for all he was worth, that this was just his way of getting back at her.

'I think we know each other now as well as we're ever going to,' she replied, belatedly, stiffly, as she felt the fingers of his one hand come to touch a stray strand of hair that lay over her shoulder.

'Oh, I wouldn't say that, my dear,' Serle murmured, no sign of the mocking note she was looking for in his voice. 'I know only the bare facts about you—I'm sure I have a lot more to learn before we . . .' he hesitated, a small cough taking him so she knew then as he choked on the words, 'er—plight our troth,' that he was sending her up for all he was worth.

'Okay, Falconer, start the car,' she told him through clenched teeth.

'Start the car?' Her hand was just itching to clout him and his phoney amazement. 'You can't mean you want me to take you home, can you? Why, I received a very clear indication from Mr Saito that you were more than willing.'

'Start the car,' Kelsey ordered grimly, her hold on her temper fast leaving.

'How can we ever get to know each other if you don't allow me private—er—converse with you?' he complained, acting it up to the hilt she was positive. 'How can we . . .'

'This has gone far enough,' Kelsey cut him off. 'Either you start this car now and take me home or . . .'

'But what will your father say?' he asked, sounding reasonable, though she thought she noted an edge coming to his tone. 'Henry was more than tactful, I thought, when he left us together for the very purpose of us finding out more about each other.'

'You know all about me that you're going to know, Falconer,' Kelsey fairly spat, and since he was insisting on bringing her father into it. 'And you can jolly well tell my father, at the very first opportunity, that you've gone off all idea of wanting to marry me too!'

She had, she recalled, noticed in him before an aversion to being bossed about by her. And that, she thought, had to be the reason for the way he stilled, let her hair fall from his hand and was momentarily as motionless as carved rock.

And when next he spoke, there was a wealth of the mockery she had been looking for. A wealth of sarcasm, as that hand moved again and he trailed the back of those fingers softly down the side of her face, then fairly fractured her, when he drawled silkily:

'Now how on earth do you expect me to tell him that, sweet Kelsey? Especially when you know as well as I do that your father is looking so much more cheerful now that I'm to be his son-in-law.'

'You . . .' she gasped, temper, anger, gone for the moment. 'What are—you saying?' she struggled, for it was one thing for her to have had the disloyal thoughts she had had, thoughts she had suspected Falconer of having too, she admitted, but quite another to have the swine bringing such thoughts out into the open.

'You don't know?' he scoffed, hardness coming to mix in with that mockery. Hardness that reminded her that her father wasn't the first parent to try and marry a daughter off to him on account of his wealth. 'Come off it, Kelsey Marchant,' he said toughly, the mockery gone, leaving only the stark hardness behind. 'You're a bright girl. If your father is as broke as you say he is, what better way to get back on his feet than to have me in the family?'

Her hand had been itching to have a go at him before. And his remark reminding her what she had told him of her father being broke, that it was only through him that her father had gambled his all, notwithstanding, in a corner through having no defence against his charges, Kelsey's only defence was to let go with her temper.

The near-darkness was no deterrent to the accuracy of her aim as her hand flew through the air and caught him. In the silence of the night, the crack of her hand against his face sounded loud to her own ears, but as she turned to find the door handle, that did not bother Kelsey one iota.

But if her other aim had been to wrench open the door and storm away from him—she was too angry then to consider that she might have set off in a totally wrong direction—she was to find that her second aim was not going to be achieved.

Hard biting hands on her arm yanked her back and the door was slammed shut before she had so much as got one foot near it. Those same biting hands twisted her round so that she had to face him again whether she wanted to or not. And his voice, as hard as his bruising hold, was grating before she could recover and hit his hands away.

'You're not thinking of going anywhere until you've allowed me to even up the score, surely?'

Still not quite recovered from finding she was not facing the way only seconds before she had been heading, not giving her time to think, she suddenly felt those hands leave her arms and come round to encircle her completely.

Too slow in realising he was going to kiss her, Kelsey began her struggles the moment his mouth touched hers. But he was strong, was Serle Falconer, as strong as she remembered from the last time he had held her in his arms. Though she did manage to pant a furious, 'Let go of me!' when he allowed her to jerk her head free, but it was to no avail. For he was kissing her again.

One kiss, for one slap, should have been good enough exchange, she fumed, getting angrier that the gear mechanism of the car was preventing her from getting a foot to him since her arms were glued by his arms to her sides. Though she did manage to get one leg over the gear system, but her kick was ineffectual and only resulted in her kimono coming open when his leg came between hers to block any more attempts.

'Stop it!' she shrieked, when as he broke his kiss to press his advantage, his body weight over her pushed her backwards so that he was lying over her.

'Like hell,' he muttered. 'You've been asking for this since that first day I saw you!'

Oh God, she thought, he's going to rape me. 'Don't!' she choked, fear, terror entering as the pressure of his body over her hardened. 'Please,' she begged, trapped, powerless to move her arms and legs so well secured by him. 'Don't—please don't!' she cried, and her voice was no longer ordering him to obey, but was begging, a high-pitched note of fear there.

Panic-stricken as she was, Kelsey was ready to fight every scrap of the way. Then, not knowing whether her terror had got through to him, or if it had never been his intention to rape her, suddenly Serle Falconer was pulling back, was pulling her to sit upright. And when she heard his voice, Kelsey had the answer to her unspoken question, it was there in his appalled-sounding:

'Good God! What sort of a man do you think I am?'

And at that moment, no thought in her when she had all the evidence she needed not to trust him, relief started to flood in, and suddenly, shaming hot tears were rolling down her face.

'Y-you—you—scared m-me,' she stammered, trying desperately to get herself together.

'Oh, hell!' she heard him grunt, then as if her tears were the living end, Kelsey felt his arm, albeit as if reluctantly, come about her. Though strangely then as he tucked her head on to his shoulder and told her, 'I meant to scare you—but not that much, I don't think,' she no longer felt afraid of his touch.

Ashamed that anyone should see her cry, she battled with her tears. 'I'm all right now,' she mumbled a minute later, still shaken, an apology hovering for crying all over him.

She made a move to sit upright, and felt him move his arm as though to let her go. Then one of his hands came to tip up her chin to see for himself what he could of the glistening in her eyes, as though he would assess for himself that she was indeed all right before he started the car.

But it was then that another strange thing happened. For with Serle Falconer looking at her, and her looking back at him, the moment seemed suddenly to be a moment suspended in time. And he, as they sat and stared at each other, appeared then to be as breathless as she. Kelsey knew that she wasn't breathing anyway. Then suddenly his mouth was over hers, and this time Kelsey wasn't struggling.

His mouth was no longer cool and exploratory, but gentle, warm and giving. And when he broke his kiss,

Kelsey wasn't thinking at all. She'd had plenty of boy-friends, had been kissed many times, but never had it felt like this.

When he pulled away from her, checked and then, just as though he had to know the feel of her mouth again, came near once more and again placed his lips over hers, Kelsey was glad. And when he pressed his body to hers, she pressed back, her arms going up and around him, as his arms were around her, his fingers gently caressing.

Again he kissed her, and again Kelsey responded, with no thought of not doing so. No thought of anything save that no man she had ever met had made her feel this way before.

Though a semblance of sanity returned when his caressing hands moved to her hip and in moving her slightly the better to get closer, his hand then trailed her thigh and with some slight feeling of shock she felt his hand under the parted material of her kimono. It was then, his movements making her clutch on to him as he caressed the warm flesh beneath his hand, that inhibiting bells in her head pealed to be heard—bells she didn't want to heed.

Her hand, going down to rest over the top of his, stayed him before his explorations progressed to being more intimate.

'No?' she heard him ask, but was unable to answer him.

She shook her head, and knew she should be glad he had received what was the right message when he brought his hand from her thigh, and cupped the side of her face.

For long silent moments he looked at her. Then a ragged sort of breath left him, and his voice was thick in his throat when he said:

'You're a heady young woman, Kelsey Marchant.'

Had she been capable of uttering a sound, she thought she might have said something very similar to him, because no man had ever had her so mindless of the criteria she had set herself before.

But as she started to come away from the emotional onslaught to her senses, she heard that Serle Falconer, too, had got a grip on the passion that had taken him. His voice was no longer husky at any rate, when next he spoke, and there was even a touch of mocking teasing there as he suggested:

'I suspect you've been kissed before?'

Yes, by you, she thought. But the kisses had never been like . . . Confused suddenly as she remembered his other kisses, kisses she had disliked as much as she disliked him, Kelsey could not comprehend how the same man could wreak such havoc in her when he tried another tack—or how she could forget for an instant how thoroughly disliked by her he was.

'I've—had my share of boy-friends,' was the best she could come up with in the shape of any answer to his question. And it suddenly dawned on her that if he thought about the way she had been with him, then unless she told him otherwise, he might read into that that there was something special in him for her; that he could make her feel that way, when nobody else ever had, 'Naturally,' she told him, 'I don't sleep with all of them.'

'Only those you're fond of?' he queried, accepting what she told him she saw, but sounding just a touch uptight, none the less.

Had she not known better, Kelsey would have thought he was sounding uptight because he was jealous. But it wasn't that, she knew. It was frustration pure and simple that, having told him that she was as liberated as the next girl, having stirred him to desire her, she had said 'No'.

'Only those I'm fond of,' she agreed. And starting to get annoyed again, perversely not liking the easy way he accepted that she slept around, 'I'd like to go home,' she added stiffly.

The key was turning in the ignition before she had finished speaking.

Serle did not attempt to kiss her goodnight as he let her off at her address, but drove away like a bat out of hell. And Kelsey went indoors in a sour mood. She knew just what was wrong with him. He had desired her, but he had had to accept that he was on a loser.

Hadn't she just told him that she only slept with men she was fond of—Serle Falconer knew he would wait till hell froze over if he waited for her to get fond of him!

CHAPTER SIX

THE Sunday that followed Kelsey's shattering discovery that against all her beliefs to the contrary, she had been in danger of losing her head over someone she was not in love with—or did not even like!—was, to say the least of it, not a happy one.

For one thing, she just could not get over the way she had been with Falconer. It haunted her, made her wonder what was wrong with her that, detesting the man, she could react to him the way she had.

That she would not be seeing him again was, from where she was sitting, the only bright spot on the horizon. Though how to tell her father that, when that morning, having, tactfully again she rather thought, been in bed when she'd got in, he was to start with fairly cheerful as he asked her how she and Serle Falconer had got on.

Not wanting to kill that look of hope in his eyes, but feeling compelled to give him some hint that this morning could well see a backtracking Mr Saito on their doorstep, Kelsey left aside that Falconer had had her emotions clamouring for more.

'We—er—didn't get on very well at all, actually,' she told him—and was stumped when he seemed to think that was quite understandable.

'A bit stilted, were you?' he nodded. And as if he thought it mattered to her, 'Don't worry about it, love. Serle's been around—he's a man of the world. I'm sure he appreciates that my little girl is shy.'

Shy! Oh lord, she thought, feeling pink, if he could have seen his little girl last night—there had been no sign of hanging back about her! 'Dad, I don't think ...' she began. Only to be interrupted by his:

'Don't worry, child. Serle will be over to see you some time today, I promise you,'

By Monday morning the hopelesst look in her father's eyes as, not wanting breakfast, he sat drinking coffee, told Kelsey since there had been no sign of Serle Falconer yesterday, that he had had to accept that when she had said things had not gone well between them, she had meant exactly that.

By that Monday too, after her father had left for work, Kelsey was able to realise that the clinging, pliable way she had been with Falconer had come about purely and simply because she was still in shock after truly believing he was going to rape her. Why, loathing him as she did, she just knew that had she been more her normal self, she would never have allowed him to lay a finger on her—much less enjoy it!

She turned her mind abruptly away from him and what he had been able to do to her, making herself concentrate on the fact that contrary to her expectations, Sunday had passed without sight or sound of Mr Saito either.

No doubt, she thought, busying herself with the housework, Falconer had been too preoccupied frying other fish to contact Mr Saito. But tonight, she knew, her father would be seeing *and* hearing from Mr Saito.

When Henry Marchant arrived home that evening, Kelsey needed to take only one look at his face to know that he was again heading for the depression that had only lifted since that first visit of the *Nakōdo*.

'Work go down all right today?' she asked, forcing brightness, when inwardly she was beside herself wondering what to do for the best.

'Not too bad,' he replied, attempting to smile, but his heart was not in it.

Turned inside out when he did little more than pick at the meal she had prepared for him, Kelsey sorely wanted to telephone her mother. She recalled how sternly he had expressly forbidden her to do so, but she couldn't help thinking that if her mother heard the whole of it, she would take the next jet out.

She sighed as, refusing to allow him to help her with the washing up, she had to reject too all idea of making that call to England.

Desperately needing his Eve as he did, he would object most strongly to her returning to Japan while he still had a mountain of debts to settle. And torn though she was, Kelsey had to know it would hurt her proud father more if she breathed a word to her mother of the utter fool he had been with his savings.

That brought Serle Falconer and his persuasive tongue to mind. But hating him as she did, Kelsey then had to face that, as proud as her father was in relation to his wife, were Falconer his son-in-law, he would see nothing wrong if Serle settled with his creditors for him.

Hanging up the tea-towel to dry, she went into the sitting room, knowing that she had to set the seal to her father's despair by coming clean before Mr Saito arrived.

'Dad,' she said, going and taking a seat beside him on the settee, 'I . . .' she broke off as the door bell chimed, and knew, as his eyes came alight in the hope that it was Falconer, that she had already left it too late. Mr Saito had arrived.

'I'll go,' she volunteered, but felt her father's hand on her arm as he got to his feet.

'You sit tight,' he said. 'You mustn't appear too eager.'

Oh God, she thought in despair of her own as he went to let Mr Saito in, this was absolutely awful!

Her eyes as bleak as her father's had been, she thought when she heard him bring Mr Saito into the sitting room that she had better raise her head to offer some form of greeting. But this was one occasion, she was thinking, when, bad form though it might be, she was going to stay by her father's side while he heard what the go-between had come to tell him. Slowly,

Kelsey looked up—and as she did, so shock took the bleakness from her eyes.

And that shock left her speechless as she blinked, and blinked again, and was still unable to believe what her eyes were telling her.

Quickly she looked from the man who, a bouquet of roses in his hands, had entered, her father with a grin from ear to ear on his face behind him. And she was still incapable of speaking when, catching her eye, her father smiled as he turned to the tall, perfectly at ease man, even without the excuse of keeping roses in his hand, and then back to her as, in quite the best humour she had seen him in of late, he beamed, obviously forgetful that he had just told her not to appear too eager.

'I told you that you had nothing to worry about, Kelsey, didn't I?' And with that grin still splitting his face, 'Serle has come courting,' he announced.

Kelsey's face went scarlet as her eyes met those of the man who had almost made her his puppet two nights ago. And observing her with a smile that was all charm, Serle Falconer thrust the roses at her.

'Hello, Kelsey my dear,' he said smoothly. 'Does your pretty colour mean you're pleased to see me?'

A month later the roses Serle had brought her were withered and dead, and Kelsey was having to take long and serious stock of what was she to do about the way Serle Falconer had become a constant visitor to the little bungalow. Though why she was pausing to take stock she didn't know, for the answer was quite simple—it was more than time she put a stop to it.

It was all down to her that she hadn't put a stop to it before it had begun, she knew that. But what with Serle at his charming and polite best, nothing in his face to reveal that a month ago he knew full well the reason for her 'pretty colour'—there was nothing wrong with his memory either of the way she had clung to him that night—and what with her father beaming so happily, she just had not been able to say to the pair of them that this had gone far enough, and that it was going no further.

She had been weak, she confessed it, but with her father once more cock-a-hoop, it had been early on that she had listened to that small voice that told her, with him pushing her at Falconer, why not go along with it? Would it hurt? Whom would it hurt? She had no idea then for how long Serle intended to play it out, but with her father's depression an established fact if she didn't go along with it, she had thought then that perhaps a week or so of her pretending she fancied Falconer might have him back on an even keel and, with his intelligence, able to see his own situation more clearly. Why, he might even be able to come up with some answer to his problems—that didn't include Falconer— some answer which had been lost to him in the fog of his unhappiness.

And so, weakened by thoughts of keeping her father's depression at bay, and thoughts of how he would be if she pushed Falconer's roses back at him and told him what he could do with them, she had gone along with it.

But that week or she had imagined it would be before Falconer got tired of his little game had stretched. It seemed incredible to her now that she had allowed it to go on for so long. Or, for that matter, that he had too.

At first she had thought she knew what it was all about. It must be, she had been convinced, that he was still out for every ounce of that pound of flesh in retribution for her insulting him as she had.

Her second thought, when a week had gone by and had seen Serle escorting her to various places of interest, culminating in a visit to his house, was that she was certain his week's 'work' was going to be concluded with him taking up from where they had left off that night in his car. For she was certain then that having that night sparked off his desire—she turned her back on the thought that it had been a mutual desire—the only reason he was dating her must be that he was a man who didn't like to have his ardour frustrated.

But. 'Shall we go?' he had said that night they had called at his home for the tickets he had for a concert but which he claimed he had forgotten.

'Go?' Wary of him, ready to thump him if he took so much as half a step to grab hold of her, 'Go where?' she asked stiffly, knowing did he have another think coming if he thought he was going to get her to go with him to any of those upstairs rooms. True, he hadn't so much as held hands with her since *that* night—but she didn't trust him. Better she trusted her instinct that told her he was waiting for something, that he had been biding his time all this week.

'The concert,' he had answered smoothly, holding the tickets aloft. And with charm coming out of every pore, a look about him that clearly told her he had read every thought in her mind, 'Had you forgotten, my dear?'

To hell with him and his 'my dear'! she had thought, shooting off the wide couch and heading out of his house, not missing the grin he wasn't quick enough to cover as she marched past him.

Last Sunday he had taken her for a long drive, and never, she thought, would she ever forget the truly wonderful scenery. Mountains of oaks and firs, deep tranquil valleys—the picture would stay etched in her mind for ever, she knew. She too had been feeling tranquil by the time Serle had pulled up at the Tededori dam. They had stood for some minutes looking at the marvellous feat of engineering with yet more tree-covered mountains in the background.

Then she had turned to him, wonder in her eyes at all she had seen. But at the look in Serle's eyes, eyes that looked down at her with warmth in them for the first time in all these weeks, so her feeling of tranquillity vanished. He's going to kiss me, she thought, and as his head came near, and her heart started hammering, she forgot completely what she was going to do to him if he so much as tried it.

But he did not kiss her. Instead he checked. And, her heartbeats still erratic, she realised it had never been his intention to kiss her as the fingers of the arm he had looked ready to place round her, went up to smooth the side of her cheek.

'You've got a smut on your face,' he said. And having wiped it away, he turned from her to suggest calmly, 'If you're feeling peckish, I know just the place for lunch.'

'I'm starving,' she had lied, for suddenly, when before she had felt she could tuck in with the best of them, she had no appetite.

Her appetite had come back later, but not the feeling of tranquillity. And as Kelsey came near to making her decision that his farcical 'courtship' had to stop, she realised that never would she feel tranquil until she had ended it.

Whatever Serle's reasons for keeping on with it—she couldn't quite remember when he had ceased to be Falconer to her and had become Serle—she could no longer fathom. But to receive another 'Who's joking'? type of non-answer should she ask him, made her refrain from putting the question.

Her reason for going out with him had been to keep her father cheerful. But now that reason had become obsolete. For her father had come so far from the depression that had dogged him that his depression was now a thing of the past.

Oh, he had had an off hour or two last week when a letter for Kelsey from her mother had been passed on via Yukiko. Her mother had made no mention of him, but because she knew he wanted to read what his wife had written but was too proud to ask, Kelsey had handed it over—he had been down for a little while then.

Serle had called for her shortly afterwards, and her

father had been in bed when he brought her home, but still with that same courteous inclination of his head Serle had thanked her politely for her company, and had bidden her goodnight.

But Henry Marchant had been his cheerful self at breakfast again. And over the next few days, Kelsey kept thinking that perhaps all separating couples went through that same tremendously bad patch in the initial stages. But they got over it, didn't they? Why, one only had to look at the second marriages one came across everywhere to know that.

Not that it was easy for her to think of her parents divorced and married to other people—they had been her ideal, and nothing in her could make her accept that. Which had her going around in circles, because other offspring had to accept that their parents were about to divorce, so why couldn't she?

Realising that the only way out of the quagmire of her thinking was to concentrate on positive thought, Kelsey saw, since there was no way her parents were going to get back together again if it was dependent on her marrying Serle, that she had to take steps, and now, to put an end to her father's hopes. He had grown stronger during this last month, but, she suddenly saw, she was doing him no favours by keeping up the pretence.

'Seeing Serle tonight?' he asked, his usual question when he came home.

Yes, but for the last time, she wanted to tell him. But she discovered that she couldn't yet be as hard as she would have to be tomorrow when she would have to tell him that it was all over.

'We're going out for a meal,' she said, and managed to tease, 'But don't worry, I've seen to it that you're catered for!'

With Serle being the same polite, charming man he had been all that month, as their meal progressed any minor qualms Kelsey experienced at the thought of his reaction when he heard what she had to say were negated by the thought that he would probably shrug his shoulders and then, with that same charm and politeness, shake hands and bid her an uncaring farewell.

Not that she wanted him to care, she thought. Good grief, that was the last thing she wanted! Though oddly, when it was such a simple thing to say, because of the circumstances no hurt on either side, they had completed their dinner and were outside the restaurant, Serle courteously handing her into the car, and she still hadn't told him.

There seemed to be more than the usual amount of traffic about, and he must be giving all his concentration to his driving, she thought, for usually he could, and often did, talk interestingly about any subject that came up. But on that drive to her home he was as silent as she was herself.

I'll tell him when he drops me off, she thought, certain she wasn't just delaying the moment. He had to give more than a little attention to the driving conditions, hadn't he? No point in distracting him unnecessarily.

But Serle, she was to discover, had already discerned that she had something on her mind. For when the car stopped outside the bungalow, he did not immediately get out and go round to the other side the way he always did. And while she was quite capable of opening car doors for herself, Kelsey found she was turning towards him, before she had thought about it. But before she could get in and tell him that this was their last date, Serle was in first, his tone even, as quietly he said:

'You've had something on your mind all evening, Kelsey,' and taking the wind from her sails, 'What's wrong?' he asked.

The ball placed squarely in her court, she suddenly felt the oddest reluctance to tell him that she didn't want to see him any more. Which had to be crazy, she thought, and she was angry enough with herself then not to hold back any longer.

'There's not a whole lot right in the way we've been so constantly seeing each other this past month, is there?' she answered snappily.

But where she was sharp, acid coming through in her tones, she realised that Serle was remaining remarkably cool, his voice even still, as he asked:

'You've found our outings boring?'

Having never thought about it, she realised that never had she experienced boredom in his company. She found him annoying sometimes, infuriating at others. But there were times when he made her laugh, times when after she had been out with him and had gone to her bed she had been near to forgetting what a farce their going out together really was—but never had she been bored. But, recollecting what this was all about before he had sidetracked her, she thought he was deliberately missing the point. And it was then, not ready to be put off by any more of his sidetracking or him being deliberately obtuse, that she came right out and told him what had been in her mind all evening.

'I'm not going out with you again,' she said, aware she was being blunt, but glad she had got it out. Though she was surprised at his short sharp answer, an edge there in his tone:

'You're leaving? You're returning to England?'

Still not having sorted out fully why he had started to take her around in the first place, she was niggled that he wasn't just accepting what she told him without question.

'Chalk up a first, Serle,' she said, her irritation finding an opening in sarcasm. 'I appreciate that you must find it shattering that a girl doesn't want to go out with you—but I'm sorry, I don't even have the excuse of a planned return to England to offer.'

In silence he accepted that she wasn't planning to leave Japan, and in silence he took her sarcasm. But when, thinking that was an end to it, Kelsey would have turned from him and opened the car door, she felt his hand come to her arm to stay her.

Knowing him well enough to know that she wasn't going anywhere until he'd had his say, she angrily shook off his hand. Her sarcasm was going to come bouncing back with a bonus, she knew that too as she moved to sit staring mutinously out through the windscreen.

But to her surprise there was no sarcasm at all in Serle's voice. Though what he said did nothing to lessen her anger, as quietly he let fall:

'You're not playing the game, my dear.'

It was that 'my dear' that did it. That phoney, phoney 'my dear'. He didn't care a button for her—not that she wanted him to, she fumed. But it was that insincere 'my dear' that had her rocketing up from merely being niggled, into exploding:

'That's all it is to you, isn't it—some game! Some game you're playing for . . .'

'It's more than a game to you?'

His quietly asked question floored her. He was making the question sound as though it was something personal to him, when she knew very well it wasn't. But she knew all about his glib tongue and then some! Why, if he'd kept his mouth shut, her poor dear father . . . It was then that Kelsey got up from the floor.

'It's a game that's too cruel to my father,' she told him shortly—angry enough not to back away from bringing into the open what all this was about anyway. 'He's up to his ears in debt, and with him believing you and I may marry, he thinks . . .' She broke off suddenly, horrified at what she was saying, even if Serle Falconer did know what was in her father's mind.

'He thinks,' he didn't blink in finishing for her, 'that with me in the family, all his financial problems will be solved.'

That edge was back in his voice, she could swear it was. And she was in there hotly to defend, 'Well, it's all your fault that he's in the fix he's in at all. If you hadn't persuaded him to invest his life's savings in some worthless scheme, he'd most likely be in England now trying to get my mother back . . .' Again she broke off, as the light from the street lamp shone on them, aware that she had all Serle's attention.

Oh God! she groaned inwardly, wanting to bite her tongue that anger had made her reveal something he was never meant to know.

'You parents have separated?'

His question was expected. But she didn't want to answer. Though as sadness hit, and sent her fury on its way, she was sure no reply was needed. Serle was shrewd enough to know anyway that with her mother being away all this time it wasn't just the legal formalities of her grandmother's estate that was keeping her.

But tears stung her eyes as he waited for his answer and she recalled what her parents' marriage had been like, and the ashes it looked like now.

'They were always so happy,' she said chokily. 'All my life I've known them as a perfect couple. They were my ideal—they had—had the sort of marriage I wanted for myself.'

A tear had slipped unnoticed down her cheek, and sudden awareness of its dampness brought her away from that softness that had settled over her. Though she refrained from wiping the tear away lest she brought his attention to it.

'Things must have started to go wrong for them before Eve was called home to her sick mother,' Serle commented.

'My—mother had wanted to return to England for some time,' she told him, guessing his logical brain had sorted that the separation had not been the result of any solitary squall. And she had to agree, 'It upset her that my father said they couldn't go—she thought he was putting his work first, so I suppose it must have grown into quite a bone of contention between them.'

'These things do rather start to snowball once they get started,' he inserted quietly, his understanding having her lost to any thought that he was her enemy. 'I can imagine it growing into quite a sizeable one, with Eve wanting to be off and Henry wanting to stay put.'

'Oh, it wasn't that he didn't want to go,' she corrected him. She smiled softly. 'He was always so proud of her, for her, it was just that he simply refused to let her standard of living drop, which it would, with his enquiries revealing that it was unlikely he would get a job in England. Or that even if he did find a job, the pay wouldn't equal the salary he's getting here—he just can't afford to go. He was too proud too,' she said sadly, 'to want her to know that at fifty-three he's on the scrap-heap as far as decent jobs go. So proud,' she ended, 'that he's forbidden me to tell her any of it.'

Lost as she was to anything save her thoughts on the sadness of her parents' break-up, Kelsey was startled into awareness that she was still sitting in the car with Serle, the lamplight playing on her face, when suddenly she felt his hand stroke down the side of her face. 'Don't cry,' he said softly, and as she felt dampness there again, only then did she realise that she had shed more than one stray tear.

'I'm sorry,' she mumbled, and ashamed he had witnessed her tears, she would have exited promptly from the car.

Only Serle's arm was suddenly about her, though it was firm and gentle as he pulled her towards him. And not sure then that her father wouldn't still be up, and not wishing him to see traces of her tears either, Kelsey allowed her head to be tucked into Serle's shoulder, as he said softly:

'It's knocked you sideways, hasn't it, to have your ideals smashed to smithereens?'

Dumbly she nodded as she fought with all she had against tears that were threatening again. 'I just can't accept—that it's all over for them,' she said chokily, strains of the tears she was trying to hold back there in her voice.

'It really hurts you, doesn't it?' said Serle softly. And Kelsey, who had no answer to make, was suddenly finding comfort in the warm mouth that settled over hers.

Her arms went round him purely because she needed something solid, secure, to hold on to. And she still needed the solidness of him, the security of him just then when Serle's mouth left hers and it appeared as though he would move away.

For Kelsey clung. And it was she who kissed him when for a moment he pulled back. Then all at once she was experiencing those same delights she had experienced with him as the master once before. Because, feeling her need, Serle did not pull back again, but for the first time in a month, he was kissing her, and it was as though he was making up for lost time.

Her head was spinning from the onslaught of his kisses. Not just kisses to her mouth alone, but to her eyes, to her throat, to the hollow between her breasts, revealed when experienced fingers did away with hook and eye after the zip on her dress, and Kelsey just clutched at him, her hands going to his hair, to his neck, around him, her hands at the buttons on his shirt.

'Sweet Kelsey,' she heard his hoarse whisper, and his hands were on the naked globes of her breasts, his body moving her willing body so that they were out of the glow of the lamplight, the pressure of him thrilling her as he half lay over her in the car.

Her breasts peaked with throbbing excitement as tender fingers planed over their sensitive tips.

'Serle,' she whispered, and was drowning her need for him.

Then suddenly, when she had thought his passion

was riding as high as the passion in her, he was stilling in his movements. But there was all the confirmation she needed as to the passion in him when, his voice ragged, he told her thickly:

'I want you, Kelsey—but not here—not like this.'

She had lost all idea of where she was, his lovemaking had done that to her. But his words, Serle putting into words his momentary physical need for her, made shock hit her at the thought of where all this had been leading. And the suggestion she thought he was making by his remark of 'not here', had her pushing at his chest.

That he not only allowed her to sit up, but helped her to do so, was another indication, she saw, that he was suggesting they went hurriedly on to his house, where he would lose no time in again getting her horizontal.

With more haste than accuracy as she slid painfully down from that state of ecstatic unawareness, Kelsey attended to the disarray of her clothes. She saw Serle wasn't bothering to do up the buttons on his shirt, and cooled another couple of degrees that he must want to resume with all speed when they reached his house.

His hand came out either to help her with her zip, or to stop her from doing it up; she was so beset by the thought of what the devil was it about this man that he could do this to her, to know for sure. But she knocked his hand away, wanting to cool down even though she was certain that she was more in control now and that nothing more was going to happen, wary of his touch that could ignite such an instant response.

Her clothing as straight as she could make it, aware that Serle was watching her, she sought for some excuse for her shocking behaviour. Shocking when she considered how she should be behaving towards him in the light of what, through him, had happened to her father.

The thought of her father and the terrible mess he was still in—all on account of Serle Falconer—was sufficient to bring Kelsey slithering the rest of the way from the pinnacle of desire Serle had taken her to. Though, annoyingly, she had to clear her throat, before she was ready.

'As a kiss of farewell, Serle,' she said, injecting all the coolness she was capable of into her tones, 'that was something else again.'

'Kiss of farewell!' he echoed, the last thing he expected to hear, she thought, dearly wishing she could see his astounded expression.

'Good heavens!' she made herself say, realising she was still shaking inside, though hoping that it wasn't showing. 'You surely don't think it was anything else!'

He moved then, and the light did catch his face. And his expression was grim, she saw, as his chin jutted forward, as well it might, she thought, beginning to feel better, since this was the second time he was going to go home frustrated.

'You're saying that all *that* was, was a pleasant *adieu* as far as you're concerned,' he grated, that threatening look there in his eyes she should have been wary of before, but hadn't been—and wasn't this time.

'You didn't think . . .!' she gasped, then paused, let the pause lengthen into two seconds, and then, never knowing she was such a good actress. 'Oh, for goodness' sake . . .' Then as if collecting herself, 'Really, Serle, you should know better. Why I told you myself I never go— all the way—unless I'm fond of the male in question.'

He had backed out of the light so she could no longer see what expression he wore. But his voice was sounding tough, when he said:

'Are you trying to tell me that had I not thought better than to take you now, and in my car, you would have been the one to stop our—interlude—before you *did go all the way?*'

Her face flared crimson. It was one thing to hope, to think, that she would have stopped him, but quite another not to know for sure. And she was as angry with herself then, as well as with him, that she couldn't be positive.

'You've been around, Serle,' she said shortly, trotting out a remark her father had once made, 'so you must know that I wasn't pretending when I kissed you back. But do you honestly believe for one moment that I would give myself to a man whom I have not only not the least liking for,' and whipping herself up into fury as she thought about it, 'but also to a man who is ultimately responsible for my parents' marriage being on the rocks!'

'You're blaming me that your parents can't make a go of it?'

His reply had been snarled, but Kelsey had not missed that he was so disdainful of wanting her liking that he hadn't bothered to mention it—though she was sure that didn't worry her, as she tore back into him.

'It's your fault that my father has lost all chance of going to England to patch things up,' she snapped. 'If it wasn't for you he would never have invested all his savings *and* money he borrowed. If it wasn't for you he might have risked going to England and finding the right job. He might . . .'

'You don't know what you're talking about,' she was cut off bluntly.

'You're saying you didn't persuade my father to invest?' she scorned, knowing very well he had.

'The mood you're in, I wouldn't dream of telling you anything,' he bit.

'Then I'll save you the bother of saying anything at all,' she said snappily. And with her hand wrenching the door open, she was through it.

But she was to find that Serle Falconer could move like lightning when he had a mind to. And that he had a mind to was obvious, for he was there beside her when she had slammed the car door shut.

'Goodbye, Falconer,' she threw at him, finality in

her tone that had that threatening glint coming to his eyes.

But he did not stop her from going up the path. And indoors, and in her bed, Kelsey had the uncomfortable feeling that it was not all over yet. For though in marching away from him she could no longer see the threat in his eyes, she had not missed that there was a threat in his voice as he had answered silkily:

'*Sayōnara,* my dear.'

CHAPTER SEVEN

OF *course* it was all over between her and Serle Falconer, Kelsey thought crossly the following morning, having time to think now that her father had left for his office. For one thing, Serle just wasn't the sort to hang his hat up to a girl where it wasn't wanted—not that he *had* been hanging up his hat, she owned, but he certainly wouldn't come back for more now that she had said goodbye.

Though having firmly decided that the threat she thought she had read in his eyes, in his tone, was all part and parcel of her being all over the place emotionally; and had she been all over the place emotionally last night! she winced, as she knew she would, her face hot as she recalled, that she'd had practically nothing on without even knowing it—well, not on her top half anyway—Kelsey found throughout that day that she just could not get Serle Falconer out of her mind.

Which was not what she wanted at all, because she wanted to give her full attention to concentrating on what she should tell her father, on how even though she had been sure he could now take it, she should tell him that she was not going to see Serle again.

But as the day wore on with her going from being cross with herself, cross with Serle Falconer, alternating with her feeling flat and lifeless, and angry too when once she had to hit firmly on the head the oddest of notions that floated through her mind, that maybe she was feeling flat and lifeless because she wasn't going to see Serle again. What a ridiculous idea, she scoffed scornfully—why, if she never saw him again it would be too soon.

But try as she would he kept coming between her and her thoughts that her father would have to be told. And told tonight, she thought, a touch of the coward coming to her to hope that if he had seen Serle that day, then maybe Serle would have told him.

One look at her father's face that night, not strained or anxious as she had seen in the past, but as happy as he could be away from his wife, and Kelsey suddenly saw that hope was still alive in him. She knew then that if his path had crossed Serle's that day, then Serle had not told him that he had received his marching orders.

'Going out with Serle tonight?' he asked, dashing all her thoughts that maybe Serle *had* told him but that feeling so much better now, he had been unaffected by the news.

'Er—no,' she said. And realising the moment was on her to tell him, she had a sudden vision of how terrible he had looked before Serle had come on the scene. Promptly she got cold feet. 'I'll go and see about dinner,' she said, and shot from her chair and into the kitchen, where she called herself all manner of cowardly names for having ducked it when the moment had been so right.

Angry with herself, she had to admit then, as she put the potatoes on to boil, that she was now not quite so certain as she had been that he was up to taking her removing that last hope from him. And as sadness invaded, taking away her anger, she knew she couldn't bear it if he returned to being the way he had been—yet on the other hand, what else could she have done but what she had? Her father had to know some time that he was living in a fool's paradise in the belief he had that Serle was going to marry her—and he *was* so much better now. Stronger than he had been.

On that thought, Kelsey knew she couldn't duck it any longer. Turning the potatoes down to a low heat, she left the kitchen and went, determined not to be so cowardly a second time, back into the sitting room where her father sat reading the paper.

'Dad,' she said, and when he looked up and saw the seriousness of her expression then put down his copy of the *Japan Times*, 'I've got something to tell you.' And sticking in there when she saw she had his full attention, 'I don't want you to be . . .' Damn, she thought, as the door bell chimed, cutting through the 'upset' she would have uttered, before she could go on with her, 'But . . .'

'You're looking very serious, love,' Henry Marchant observed. 'I'll answer the door first, shall I? Then you can tell your old dad what's troubling you uninterrupted.'

Feeling her strength deserting her, Kelsey willed it back as he left the room. She had the dreadful suspicion that he was going to be looking far more serious, far more troubled than she was when their conversation was over.

Anger to hear two pairs of footsteps returning had her flagging courage returning. If Serle Falconer had called, ignoring that last night she had definitely said goodbye to him, then even if it had to be done in front of her father, she was again going to tell him the same thing—with emphasis!

It was not Serle who came first into the sitting room. And for one moment Kelsey was left wondering what she was thinking about to imagine he would call anyway. For the next instant of seeing that their caller was none other than Mr Saito, she was realising that Serle had indeed taken her at her word.

'Would you get some refreshment for our guest, Kelsey?' Henry Marchant asked. And certain it wasn't disappointment she felt at the realisation that, having sent the go-between to begin negotiations, Serle, very correctly, had sent him to terminate them, Kelsey went into the kitchen to do her father's bidding.

Though she was quickly back in the sitting room with the glass of wheat tea she had learned how to make and which she thought the go-between would prefer. And her glance went quickly to her father to see how he was taking what Mr Saito was telling him.

He couldn't have got started yet, she thought, placing the *mugi cha* in front of their guest along with a couple of tiny cakes. For though he was doing most of the talking, she guessed, since her father was beaming broadly, that Mr Saito was going through the pleasantries first.

Probably discussing baseball, Japan's number one sport, she thought. But she was determined then that, unlike the other time, this was a time when she was staying. Even if she couldn't understand a word of what was being said, she was staying. Not that she would need a translation; she knew well enough what Mr Saito had come to say before her father relayed it in English.

The oddest thing was, though, that in the whole of the time that the go-between was talking, not once did her father's happy look leave him.

She recalled the threat that had been in Serle's eyes, that threat that said she hadn't heard the last of him yet. But she shrugged that away, the way she had shrugged it off that morning. It *was* over. It *was* finished with. It was just that her father, so much better now, was able to mask any upset he was feeling by a polite smile.

She had her own *'Sayōnara'* to say to Mr Saito when finally he stood up to take his leave. And while her father saw him out, and she waited for him to return, she sat eyeing the small white parchment-looking parcel bound with gold and silver twine in a fancy shape, and with an artificial flower in one corner, which Mr Saito had left behind.

Perhaps it contained a formal declaration of the nullification of the proceedings, she thought, not having an idea how such terminations were usually performed. But hearing her father's step, she left such wonderings and prepared herself to meet any of the questions he would put as to why had he to wait for Mr Saito to tell him when she had seen him at breakfast and in the time since he had been home this evening.

'No wonder you were looking serious, love,' he said, coming back into the room, that broad smile still on his face. 'You tried to tell me before our visitor called, didn't you?'

'Er—yes,' she answered, her brow puzzled. Something was wrong, she just knew it was. She wanted her father happy, of course she did, but he was taking it too well. 'I was afraid—er—afraid you might be upset,' she murmured.

And all at once she was on the receiving end of a sincere and fatherly hug from her parent, who kissed her cheek, then stood back to look at her, his face unsmiling for a second as he said:

'Well, no father really wants to part with his little girl.' And a grin he couldn't contain burst out again as Kelsey sought desperately to discover what he was talking about. 'But I have no anxieties about handing you over to Serle's safe keeping.'

'Serle's safe keeping!' she echoed faintly, her voice choked, but finding he was in such high spirits, that he just wasn't seeing her exclamation as being one of surprise.

'As soon as Mr Saito passed that over I knew,' he said, his eyes going from her to the decorated parcel that lay on the table.

'You knew?' she questioned, and, floundering, 'What is it?' she asked.

'It's your *yuino*,' he beamed, going over to the commercially prepared package and handing it to her. Then shattering her completely, he explained, 'Serle has as good as said he wants to marry you by sending that along.'

And she thought she had been floundering before!! Anger was building up in her that she hadn't been mistaken, that she hadn't imaged that 'you haven't

heard the last of me' glint in Serle Falconer's eyes, and
she was still looking dumbfounded enough for her
father, catching her expression, to pause and then decide
why it was she was looking as if she didn't fully
understand what was going on.

'Of course,' he said cheerily, 'you can't have heard of
the *yuino*.'

'Er—no, I haven't,' she agreed, her right hand
starting to itch to come into contact with a certain
person—he *was* up to something.

'It's the custom here,' Henry Marchant explained,
'and since Serle has done his courting according to the
customs of the country he's in, why shouldn't an
engaged girl receive what they call *yuino* from her fiancé
in advance of the wedding?'

Well, Serle Falconer was going to have it straight
back, whatever it was! Kelsey thought. Her father
obviously thought she saw now that the something she
had to tell him was that Serle had proposed. And if that
wasn't enough to set her hate going—she was back to
hating Falconer with everything she had when her
father went on to explain exactly what *yuino* was.

It was money. Money given before marriage by the
fiancé of the bride-to-be, in order for her to buy such
furniture and fittings as was thought necessary for their
future home. About one million yen was the usual sum,
so he said. But as Kelsey did a rapid calculation and
translated that amount into somewhere over two
thousand pounds, so her eyes started to go wide, and he
was ending:

'Though I shouldn't be surprised, since Serle had no
need to save his coppers to be able to raise that amount,
that your *yuino*, Kelsey, will far exceed that sum.'

Her yuino! Blisteringly angry, she wished she knew
where Mr Saito lived so she could take that package
straight back to him.

'Aren't you going to open it?'

She was brought away from her outraged thoughts at

her father's question. She looked from the package in her hands, the word 'No' there, then the word died on her tongue. Because, shaken rigid, she could see that he was not looking at her, but at the package. And much though she didn't want to believe what her eyes were telling her, as clearly as if he had said it, she was reading in his eyes the hope that some of what the package contained would be finding its way to him!

'Come on, love, don't keep me in suspense,' he urged, and it was obvious that he was in suspense to see how much there was for him, not her.

'I don't . . .' she tried.

Then all of a sudden, her heart softened. The poor dear love, she thought, he wasn't avaricious, she knew he wasn't. All that was driving him, all that was making him forget that the money had been sent for her, not for him—if indeed the package contained money—was his burning need to be reunited with her mother. And all he could see was that maybe the package contained the means of that reunion being accomplished.

Hardly aware of what she was doing, Kelsey slipped the gold and silver band from around the parchment—the artificial flower falling unheeded to the floor. Then piece by piece she undid each flap of the parcel until she was holding in her hands the bulky envelope at its centre. Having gone too far then to flinch now, she opened the envelope and extracted the contents.

Minutes later both she and her father were still sitting on the settee where first one and then the other had slumped to, the money in a pile between them.

'Twenty thousand pounds,' said Henry Marchant, the way he had a couple of times since the envelope had been opened, though his voice sounded less hoarse this time.

And he was then giving her the broadest of hints, as looking away from her, as though slightly ashamed of himself, but his need of the money far greater than hers:

'I've been to Serle's house a time or two, as you

have,' he said quietly. And as Kelsey looked down and saw that his knuckles were showing white, 'Serle has a houseful of beautiful furniture already, hasn't he, love?'

'Yes,' she agreed on a whisper, being torn in two inside. She should tell him that that money had to go back, that there was not the smallest likelihood of her and Serle marrying. She should tell him, and now, she thought, that only last night she had told Serle that she wasn't going to see him again. But as she looked again at his white knuckles, she heard too the unbearable tension in him, the strain in his voice, as he said:

'Then don't you think the *yuino* he has sent for you must be Serle's way of saying he wants you to have the money as a personal gift from him to you?' No, no, she didn't think that at all, she wanted to tell him. But he was pressing his theme, 'The type of package Mr Saito brought is always the sort used when money is presented as a gift. By sending a *gift* envelope, Serle must mean for you to do with the money whatever you wish.'

'Dad,' she croaked, wanting to tell him he couldn't have it, that it wasn't hers to give. 'Dad,' she said chokily again, and would then, she thought, have been able to deny him his happiness. *Would*, she thought, have been able to, had he not chosen that precise moment to take his eyes from whatever object across the room they were focussed on and turn them to look at her.

And what Kelsey saw there in those moist pleading eyes was the look of a man about to die if she took this last chance away from him. And it was her hands which were clenched then, her knuckles which were white as she fought to deny him the chance to live against what everything else inside her was screaming—that the money was not hers to give, that it should be sent back to its owner with all speed.

She was not conscious of having made a decision as she picked the money up from the settee. She was conscious only that he would be able to accept it with less shame, if he thought she was giving it to him willingly.

'What the heck do I want with twenty thousand pounds?' she said, a smile on her face that was at odds with the deep unhappiness inside her, as she pushed the money at him.

'Oh, Kelsey—oh, love,' he said, a proud man who had come near to the bottom. 'What can I say?'

'Just be happy,' she told him, and there were tears shining in her eyes as she added, knowing he needed a fillip to his pride, 'What's twenty thousand between friends—you're a great dad, you know.' And when for the second time in her life she thought she was going to see him weep, and she just couldn't take that, briskly, brightly, she asked, 'Now, who's going to ring Mother, you or me?'

Once she had mentioned her mother, all other thought left Henry Marchant but to break the silence with his wife that seemed to have gone on for ever.

Kelsey busied herself in the kitchen while he telephoned. She guessed their conversation would have no room for her, though she could speak to her mother another time. Serle Falconer, the money he had sent, both tried to get into her head, but she didn't dare allow herself to think about him or his money. The die was cast, too late to wonder if she had done the right thing!

Her father coming to find her in the kitchen half an hour later—that phone call was going to cost a bomb!—his eyes shining like those of a small excited schoolboy, were all she needed to know that Serle's money had been well spent and that her father's phone call had been well received. Though for all, in her father's eagerness, he had forgotten about the time change and he had been lucky to catch Eve in the middle of the day. Then he was slapping his forehead, an indication that he had forgotten something else too.

'I didn't say a word about you and Serle!' he suddenly remembered.

'I should be surprised if I got a mention at all,' Kelsey grinned, in the face of his utter and sublime happiness. 'Is a mere daughter allowed to know what's going on?' she enquired, able to tease, able for the moment to keep the door tight shut on thoughts that were going to have her sleepless when she let them in.

'Like what, for instance?' he replied, teasing in turn, suddenly, all at once, the laughing-eyed father she had always known.

'Like are you going to be welcomed back into the fold?'

'I wondered about that myself before I phoned,' he said seriously, and confessed, 'I've been terrified Eve would have found somebody else before I could get to her.'

'Oh, Dad!' she reproached him, though realising that although she had asked her mother herself if there was anybody else, that her father, not seeing the two of them through her eyes, must have had all manner of such thoughts going through his head.

'I know,' he said. 'Crazy, wasn't I? Anyway, I simply told Eve that I couldn't live without her any longer.'

'And what did she say?'

'Want to know it all, don't you?' He was back to teasing again.

'Only the uncensorable bits,' she said cheekily.

'Remind me to give you a talking to some time,' he came back, but went on to reveal that Eve had told him it was about time he realised that she had more charms than his stuffy office.

With Henry Marchant in top form now that all his hopes were to be realised, their delayed meal and the rest of the evening passed with him at his most talkative. In a serious moment he told Kelsey that, life being no life at all without her mother, the standard he had set himself had paled, so that had it not been for the debts that were hanging around his neck—it had made a difference that Eve had inherited Gran's home, since the headache of where would they live and how much such accommodation would cost, relieved—he would have given serious thought to leaving Japan and taking his chances of being able to find a decent job when he got to England.

On the one hand overjoyed for him that Serle's money would settle all his debts in Japan and still leave him a tidy sum to tide him over until he got himself sorted out in England, Kelsey at last went to bed no longer able to hide from facing all the terrible minuses on the other hand.

With no thought in her head of going to sleep she undressed and lay on top of her mattresses that hot night; and was then bombarded by a whole host of questions, that started with a very enormous first one. What had she done? Just what dreadful, dreadful thing had she done?

Her heart went bumping wildly at the insane thought—did Serle really want to marry her; was that why he had sent the *yuino*? Of course he didn't want to marry her, came back the answer; and her heart settled to a dull thud as she realised the truth of that reply.

So why on earth had he sent Mr Saito with twenty thousand pounds? Not chickenfeed by anyone's standards, even his, she would have thought. Oh, why, why, why had he sent it?

Kelsey was still searching for an answer the next day. That her father had spent a sleepless night too, though it had been happy excited thoughts that had kept him awake, she knew, was evidenced by his tired though at-peace-with-the-world eyes.

'Morning, love,' he greeted her, coming into the kitchen and yawning widely.

'Sleep well?' she asked, finding a teasing note from somewhere.

'Too much on my mind,' he replied happily, and

Kelsey had a feeling then that, up there on cloud nine, should one of Japan's not infrequent earthquakes happen today, he wouldn't even notice it.

The lighthearted manner she tried to keep up to match his, even the prospect facing him of telling his employers that he was breaking his contract not daunting him, fell away from Kelsey the moment she had waved her father off. And she was again in the swirling nightmare of thoughts that, contrary to her hope, hadn't lightened at all with the coming of day.

It was less than useless to repeat what had gone through her head in the dark hours of the night; that she had come to Japan with the specific aim of doing something to get her parents back together again, and that having achieved precisely that aim, it was no use crying about the way her aim had been achieved—Serle Falconer was twenty thousand pounds the lighter!

Oh lord, why had he sent that money? Why had he put that temptation in her way? And again she was plagued with the thought, why, why had he done it?

Over the past month she thought she had grown to know a little about him; but suddenly she found she was asking herself the question—could Serle have learned to know a little about her? Had he seen in her that something that in view of what she had told him the last time she had seen him made him realise that she would give his money to her father! She stayed with the thought.

She had, after all, told him it was his fault that her father was broke, that he was the cause ultimately of her parents' separation. Had she perhaps got through to his conscience? Did he, in fact, have a conscience?

Oh, grief, she thought, her mind cavorting like a roundabout, what was the answer? Was Serle not feeling any compunction at all for what he had done when he had persuaded her father to make that unwise investment? Or was this Serle's way of having the last word? Was he perhaps angry that, possibly for the first time in his life, some female had been the first to say, I've had enough, that he had chosen this way to make believe it was he who was concluding the episode, this his way of putting the final seal to it? A colossally expensive final seal, surely?

By the time her father was due home from his office that night, Kelsey had run herself ragged. All through the day she had tortured herself with trying to find the answers to questions to which there just were not any answers—not unless she went to see Serle and got the answers from him. Which raised yet another question— was Serle expecting her to get in touch with him? Kelsey was then assaulted with new thoughts she didn't want— surely it was up to her to go and see him, or, alternatively, up to her to send that money back.

When Henry Marchant, as cheerful-looking as he had been that morning, walked through the door, Kelsey's mind had just lit again on the absurdity of the thought—it would look well if Serle had sent the money because, intending to stay on in Japan, he wanted an English wife; and intended to marry *her!* So she was more than pleased to see her father, because his presence there prevented her wild imaginings from going any further.

'How did it go?' she asked. 'Were they angry with you for breaking your contract?'

'Polite and inscrutable as I expected,' he told her. And with his grin showing, making up for its sombre replacement when she had first arrived, 'But guess what?' Kelsey shook her head and waited, having no idea. 'Because I tried to stick to the truth wherever possible, and told them I must return to England because as delightful as my wife finds Japan, she wishes to remain in England, and that therefore I must join her; I've been told that while they're not promising anything, they'll look into the possibility of a vacancy for me in the U.K. branch.'

'Why, that's marvellous!' Kelsey exclaimed.

'They're not promising, mind,' he warned. 'Though the hint was dropped that it wouldn't be a bad idea to have someone who can read, write and speak Japanese at the other end. Meantime, and in view of me not wanting to blot my copy book any further, when they asked me to stay on for a month, I said I would.'

'You'd better ring Mother,' said Kelsey, seeing that if her mother was getting excited at the idea of him being home within the week, as had been the way he had been talking last night, then she ought to be told straight away.

'I've done that already. I rang her after I'd nipped out to make my flight arrangements,' he said making her aware that the twenty thousand had already been dipped into for his ticket. And then, as if he was looking for plusses, he told her, 'The few extra weeks will give me more time to settle my affairs here.' By that she guessed he meant his creditors. Then came the question she had been waiting for. 'Seeing Serle tonight?'

'He rang,' she lied, a chink already appearing in that money; there was no point in giving her father food for thought that not to see her intended two nights in a row looked peculiar, especially when Serle lived only a quarter of a mile away. 'He's got some business he's tied up with at the moment and can't get out of.'

'He never stops, does he?' said her father admiringly, accepting without question what she had told him.

The following day saw Kelsey again chasing for answers she had sought all the previous day. But on top of that was the greatest agitator of all, for that question her father's timely arrival had stemmed was there again in full force to haunt her. Did Serle mean to marry her?

Sure that he did not want to marry her any more than she wanted to marry him, but getting panicky nevertheless, Kelsey gave thought to returning to England with her father. But it was then that in deciding to return to England with him, she came up against a gigantic brick wall in opposition to that idea.

For, with him taking that money from her *only* because he thought she was going to marry Serle, how *could* she return to England with him? Her father's pride would never surface again if she now told him that she wasn't going to marry Serle! Why, what with daily interest rates being what they were, in all probability her father had spent some of yesterday in not only booking his ticket home, but in visiting his bank and settling with at least one of his creditors!

A groan she couldn't stifle broke from her then. For all at once it became startlingly clear to her that with the twenty thousand already broken into, if she told him that Serle was not going to be his son-in-law, then her father would look on Serle as another of his creditors. And that far from achieving her aim in coming to Japan, all she would have succeeded in doing would be to get her father yet deeper into debt than he had been before!

Believing she'd had enough on her mind to be going on with, Kelsey discovered there was still more that could go wrong. For it was over their meal that night that her father told her he had been along to Serle's office that day for a 'chat', only Serle had been tied up with some bankers.

'I'll see if I can catch him tomorrow,' he added. 'Though with his negotiations on the boil, I may not be lucky.'

That he had not asked was she seeing Serle that night, assuming she guessed that Serle was still busy with the business she had invented that had kept him occupied last night, was a relief to her. In truth her powers of invention were fast drying up, as she waded in the quagmire of how was she going to prevent her father—when he worked in the same building—of seeing and talking to Serle before his plane took off on the first leg of his journey for England. And not only that—how, for goodness' sake, was she going to excuse Serle not coming to the house, or her not going out with Serle for the remaining weeks before her father left?

The idea occurred to her of taking herself off each night and coming home to say she had been out with Serle, but the idea had to be scrapped; there was little chance of it working. Her father was bound to think it funny that not only did Serle not pop in for a moment, but that he never heard his car—and there was still the problem of the two of them working in the same building. It was unlikely, even as busy as Serle was, that with his office only up the hall from her father's they wouldn't bump into each other accidentally, even without her father going to seek Serle out.

Her problems were occupying her so thoroughly that Kelsey nearly jumped out of her skin when the telephone rang.

'Answer that, Kelsey, will you?' called her father in the middle of having a sort out in his bedroom in preparation for his packing. 'I've got my hands full at the moment, but I'll be there in a tick.'

It went without saying that the call would be for him, but it would let the caller know that someone was at home, even if they didn't understand her English when she asked them to hold on.

But Kelsey was to find that not only was her English understood, but that she didn't have to ask anyone to hold on while her father came to the phone. For the telephone call was not for him, but for her.

'I know you were going to give me a ring some time tonight,' said Serle, his brand of sarcasm as fine as ever and having her eyes flicking to the clock that said it had gone nine-thirty, 'but I thought I'd save you the trouble.'

Colour rushed to her face, ashamed colour that, although she had taken his money, Serle obviously thought it a shade off that not so much as a thank-you had he received.

'Er—hello, Serle,' she stammered, embarrassed, hot under the collar that her father had come into the room and was standing watching her.

There was silence at the other end which made her hope her father thought that Serle was saying something, for not prepared for this moment, though belatedly realising that she should have been—her brain had seized up.

'It occurred to me,' Serle went on when the possibility of her standing there mute clenching on to the phone for the rest of the evening looked likely, 'that a serious talk between us wouldn't come amiss. *Tonight*,' he added in a voice there was no arguing with.

Panic in an instant made her nerve ends jangle. 'I'll come round,' she said quickly, her anxiety rampant that he and her father would meet.

'I have no objection to coming to see you.'

Swine, she thought, he knew damn well she was in a blue funk! 'I fancy the walk,' she managed, keeping her tone sweet.

But her rebellion disappeared, as did her colour, when the line went dead. Her father was looking at her with that pleased look in his eye that told her he thought it only natural that Serle should ring her the moment that his business was through. That he thought it only natural that they should want to see each other whatever the hour. Oh, help me, somebody! she cried inwardly. Serle was insisting, it had been there in that unarguable with '*Tonight*.'

Blue funk wasn't the word for it, she thought, as she realised that if she didn't get her skates on, Serle would not hesitate to come to seek her out for that 'serious talk'. Oh God, she thought, panic-stricken, what the dickens was she going to do if he asked for his money back?

CHAPTER EIGHT

Kelsey's insides were all knotted up as she stood waiting for Serle to open the door in answer to her ring. All the way to his home the one major thought that had dominated was the same one that had rocked her when she had replaced the phone after his call—just what was she going to do if he asked for his money back?

'You didn't hang about, I see,' he said for openers, as he stood back from the door to let her in.

'I never was one to dawdle,' she replied stiffly, edgily, not having been able to outrun her thoughts no matter how she had hurried.

Serle led the way into the large airy sitting room she had been in before, her eyes taking in the well furnished room, an endorsement there that apart from perhaps a few feminine touches; there would be no need to spend any of that twenty thousand on another stick of furniture.

Not that the money had been sent for that purpose, she thought angrily, when she had decided on her way here that she wasn't going to get angry; that she wasn't going to get uptight either.

'Drink?'

Unaware he had been watching her, Kelsey glanced to where Serle stood over by a drinks cabinet. She saw he was looking cool and at ease. And why wouldn't he be at ease? she thought sourly; the deck was stacked in his favour.

'No,' she said shortly, adding, 'thanks,' as an afterthought. She wanted this interview over and done with quickly.

'Then may I invite you to take a seat?' he enquired, his eyes still watchful as, deciding against a drink for himself, he left the cabinet and strolled casually towards her.

Swine, she thought again, and she was as angry with herself as much as him then. For as he neared her and she looked into his strong face, looked into those ever watchful eyes, her heart suddenly set up a thunderous beating. And for the first time ever, there was no heat in her when thinking him the swine he was.

Abruptly she turned, confusion rioting in her, confusion that had started up from just looking at him.

'That money,' she said, and her voice was suddenly husky as she came blurting out with the crux of her visit, when maybe it would have been better to have arrived there more slowly. Kelsey swallowed hard, then thought she had herself under control. And having got the ball rolling, she turned to face him and asked him point blank, 'Did you send that money because you wanted the last word?'

'Last word?' he repeated. But she wasn't fooled that he didn't know what she was on about. And she was glad of the anger that returned to her then, because though she hadn't wanted it before—*now* she needed it.

'You've been trying to make me pay ever since I insulted you in that restaurant that day,' she challenged hotly. 'You can't deny it.'

Her remark, her challenge, had irritated him. She could see that by the way his mouth firmed and his cool air deserted him. But he wasn't denying her accusation.

'I never was one to leave accounts unsettled,' he replied shortly.

'So I *was* right,' Kelsey challenged again. 'The accounts weren't balanced, to your way of thinking. I was the one who put an end to the farce of our seeing each other.' Kelsey saw from the narrowing of his eyes, from the coldness in his look, that she should stop there. But she was too wound up to stop until she had finished. 'You sent Mr Saito with that money purely and simply because *you* wanted to be the one to end it. You wanted me to squirm, didn't . . .'

'Squirm?'

He sounded surprised at her use of the word, but she wasn't fooled. 'You sent that money hoping I would spend it, just for the pleasure you would get of seeing me wriggle when you asked for it back,' she flared, in the heat of the moment bringing out a thought that had just occurred to her.

Though had it been his intention to see her wriggle, then she was very sure she wasn't going to, and in answer to his terse, 'You sound as though you have spent it?' she didn't flinch either when smartly on the heels of that, he asked bluntly, 'Have you spent it?'

Hot all over as she felt, Kelsey just refused to let him see her squirm. 'Your money has gone,' she told him outright.

But she came near to hitting him a third time as she saw the way he received her stony offering. For she could have sworn she saw triumph in his eyes, masked though that triumph quickly was, concealed as it quickly was as he changed his mind about having that drink and, without commenting, wandered over to the drinks cabinet.

Kelsey had control of her urges, when, holding a Scotch in his hand, taking her at her word that she didn't want a drink and not repeating his offer, he returned to scan her face thoughtfully. Though she still wasn't of a mind to start squirming when his question came, as she knew it would, of how was she going to pay him back.

But to her surprise, though it was a question he put to her, that was not what he asked. Though before asking anything, cool again, he took a swig from the glass in his hand. He raised his eyes to her defiant face. Then quietly he dropped out:

'When is your father leaving?'

'I . . .' she stumbled, shock hitting her that he knew

without asking on what the money had been spent. Hastily she pulled herself together. 'My father hopes to have his affairs settled within the month,' she replied—and was back to hating him, as he took another swig from his drink, his expression no longer cool, but stern, hard, and not very likeable, as he questioned:

'He has some idea of you going with him?'

Her father hadn't given the idea any thought whatsoever, though, loath though she was to say so, Kelsey saw that the time had gone when prevarication would have fitted.

'Well?' he barked, making her more uptight to be spoken to that way—by him—even if he didn't take kindly to being kept waiting; the inquisition was his.

'He hasn't asked me to go with him,' she said tautly. And, angry lest he thought it a strange state of affairs, or that her father didn't love her, 'He thinks I'm staying behind to—to marry you.'

Serle finished the rest of his drink in one swallow. Then he was looking her full in the eyes as silkily, after a moment's pause, he murmured, 'And you, Kelsey—you think that you're not?'

Colour flooded her face. But she wasn't sure then that her colour was all from the fury that surged through her at the cat-and-mouse game he was delighting in. But suddenly her emotions—on one gigantic see-saw ever since she had arrived in Japan, or so it seemed—erupted, and everything in her went wild. And to her utter consternation, she heard herself yelling:

'To hell with you, Falconer! Tell me plainly—do you want to marry me or . . .' she broke off, gasping. She had meant to challenge what the hell did he mean by '—you think you're not?' But, stunned by what she had just asked, she was still gasping when she heard him laughing at her!

He had laughed at her before, but this time it was just too much. This time she really couldn't take it. And it had gone beyond wanting to hit him—Kelsey was on her way even as the pleasure in him abated sufficiently for him to reply sardonically:

'Now that's a nice a proposal as I've ever had.'

As she had told him, she never had been one to dawdle, and with his mocking words still ringing in her ears, Kelsey had slammed the front door shut behind her, her feet sprouting wings.

Her feet flying, she was near to tears that she could not escape the thoughts that chased after her. Oh God, she thought, oh God! When Serle had only been tormenting her about marriage, his engaging Mr Saito being just his way of getting even with her, what had she done—even if it was in temper—she had only asked him outright if he wanted to marry her, that was all!

A stitch in her side, tears blinding her, Kelsey had to slow down. But she was still sorely mourning what she had said. To her way of thinking, it wouldn't have hurt half as much to have her proposal laughed at if only that night—if only that night in Serle's house she had not discovered that she—was head over heels in love with him.

'You're soon back!'

Her father's greeting made her aware that she had not given one thought to him since she had rocketed from Serle's house. Had she done so, she might have thought to put on a bright face before she went in. Too late now, he had seen her flushed face and pink-rimmed eyes, and he was coming over to her and exclaiming:

'What's wrong, love? You've been crying!'

'I—er—had a row with Serle.' The admission was out before she could stop it. And that didn't surprise her either, for never had she felt so confused in her life. How could she be in love with a man who was responsible for all the suffering her father had been through?

'I'll make you a cup of tea,' said Henry Marchant.

And Kelsey wanted to cry again that he should think that a cup of tea would put everything right.

She was still in a confused state when, patting her sympathetically on her shoulder as he passed, her father placed a cup of tea in front of her. It did nothing to lift her confusion when he said:

'Don't fret, love, Serle will soon be round to make it up.' She didn't answer—she doubted if Serle would stop laughing long enough to remember where she lived. 'Come on, chick,' he coaxed, 'cheer up! I know you love him and that you're upset now, but . . .' he checked, but only momentarily as he saw a spasm take her, 'but you know you can trust him not to . . .'

'Trust him!' was jerked from her.

'Of course—trust him,' he replied. And, still trying to tease her out of her unhappiness which he saw as nothing more than her being upset after a lovers' tiff, 'Do you think your old dad would let you marry him if he didn't trust him too?'

Grappling with her confusion, it came to Kelsey that she could not tell him that she wasn't going to marry Serle, not if she didn't want all her father's plans to go up in smoke she couldn't. But, still highly emotional, she just couldn't refrain from saying bitterly:

'I just don't know how you can still trust him after what he did to you.'

'What he did to me?' His exclamation made her lift her head to look at him. And she knew yet more confusion that he appeared as astounded as he had sounded, as he asked, 'What on earth are you talking about? Why, I've never come across a more highly principled man than Serle. His integrity is second to none.'

High principles? Integrity? Serle? 'But . . .' she choked, remembering that day she had arrived to find him hitting the bottle, 'it was Serle who persuaded you to put everything you could in that unsound investment! He persuaded you when he knew all the time that it wasn't worth a light.' In the face of her father's utter astonishment, her voice had started to peter out. 'You told me so yourself,' she managed to add, her voice taking a higher note. Her confusion was complete when, forcefully, her father replied:

'*That* I never did!'

'Yes, you did,' she argued quickly. 'You told me that day I arrived that you had Serle to thank that you no longer had your nest egg.'

She saw he was trying to remember back to that day, when, being the worse for drink, he would have been incapable of inventing untruths. And she guessed when, his memories as complete as they ever would be of that day, that he was only trying to whitewash Serle because he wanted her to see only good in the man he thought she was going to marry, when he at last said:

'I was at a low ebb then—and, unfairly I admit now, ready to blame anybody but myself for my own stupidity.'

'You were desperate then, not stupid,' she reminded him.

'Desperate *and* stupid,' he amended. 'But Serle didn't know anything of my personal circumstances. Had he any idea that in order to get rich quick I would invest my all, and then some, he would have telephoned me immediately, the way he did the others.'

She didn't believe him, but found her curiosity stirring sufficiently to ask, 'What others?'

'I'll start at the beginning,' said Henry Marchant, observing that her confused look wasn't being helped any by her having to try and fill in the blanks he had left out. 'I suspect the version I gave you before was slightly—rambling.'

'A little,' she agreed, minimising the way he had been, for his pride's sake.

'Well, to start with, I heard whispers of this investment which everyone with an eye to business was considering. But even with your mother wanting to return to England and there being no way financially that I could manage it, I was too cautious to want to invest myself.'

That sounded truthful, more like him. He was normally a very cautious man. That was why she just knew someone else had to be at the back of his ignoring that steady caution.

'However,' he went on, 'that didn't stop me keeping my ears open. By then we'd had your letter about Gran getting worse, and I could see what was going to happen if the next thing we had was a phone call.'

'That Mother would go to England, and might not come back.'

'No might about it,' he said, and resumed. 'Anyway, the next day rumours about the investment were hotting up, and it was then I began to wonder if I was being over-cautious—I could certainly do with a quick return for my money, I thought . . .' He was reflective for a moment, then he continued, 'I think I must already have been teetering on the brink when after some business function, with all the top brass there, I overheard Serle, whose judgement I've always valued,' he inserted, 'telling the top brass that he was going to invest.'

With all her heart Kelsey wanted to believe that that was all the extent of Serle's involvement had been, that that was all his persuasion had been. But even with her father now looking so sincere that she had to know he was speaking the truth, she just had to question:

'But you told me that he'd let you invest, yet had no intention of investing himself?'

'I can't remember now exactly what I did tell you,' he replied, looking shamefaced in apology. 'But after hearing Serle saying he was going to invest, I was so busy wondering, should I, shouldn't I, and from where could I get the biggest loan to make my investment larger if I did—I wasn't in the group he was with, remember—that I didn't hear him tell the others that in view of the whole thing having to be kept quiet, he intended to fly to Tokyo the next day to make a few discreet enquiries.'

'That same day as Mother flew out from Komatsu,' said Kelsey, remembering him saying Serle had taken that same plane.

'That's right,' he nodded. 'The night before the phone call I'd been dreading came through from you.' His face went bleak for a moment, but not for long as he remembered that in a month's time he too would be in England. 'Mistakenly, when I went to see your mother off and saw Serle at the airport, I convinced myself that he was Tokyo-bound to release as much of his private capital as he could, and at the same time be on the spot to get in on the ground floor with his own investment.'

'Oh, Dad,' Kelsey cried, seeing it all, 'you must have been horrified when you heard you'd lost all your money!'

Horrified was an understatement as he went on to reveal how distraught he had been, with Serle back in Komatsu, to hear some of the directors warmly thanking him for his tip-off phone call from Tokyo advising them not to touch the investment. Quickly he had tried to disguise how he was feeling, but Serle had suddenly spotted him, and noticing how sick he was looking had come over to ask if he was all right. He had said he was fine, but hadn't been able to stop himself from remarking that he had thought he had overheard him saying that he was going to invest.

'If I'd heard that, Serle told me, then I must have heard him add "but only if it stands up to my private enquiries".'

'But you didn't hear him add anything?' prompted Kelsey, not needing his shake of his head.

'My mind had taken off to wonder why, with Serle going for it, was I dithering when I should be acting while the going was good. Anyway, Serle was then looking at me in some astonishment, and was asking, "You didn't go in, did you?" '

Kelsey remembered her first meeting with Serle that day she had charged into his office. He had looked incredulous then too when she had told him that her father had made that investment—and she had thought his incredulity all so much sham! Groaning inwardly, she knew the answer to her next question too before she asked it.

'You told him you hadn't?'

'My money had gone—too late to do anything about it. It was one thing to know myself for a fool, quite another to let anyone else know it, especially Serle, for whom I have the greatest respect. So I told him no, and excused the way I knew I must be looking on the worry I had on my mind about what was happening in England with Eve's mother being so ill.'

'And Serle accepted that?'

'It was logical. He'd journeyed on the same plane with Eve as far as Tokyo—they'd probably spoken about why she was going.'

Kelsey looked sadly at her father. 'Thank you for telling me all that,' she said simply, quietly, he squeezed her hand affectionately, as he said:

'So you see, love, the man you're going to marry is entirely honourable, entirely trustworthy.' And, smiling now as he tried to encourage a smile from her, 'Had Serle any inkling that cautious old Henry Marchant was so much as thinking of investing, he would have told me too to hold fire until he'd made his enquiries. And I too would have received a telephone call from Tokyo.'

Lying sleepless that night, Kelsey saw she had an awful lot of apologising to do to Serle Falconer. Oh, how right her heart had been—how wrong her head.

Would he laugh at her again if she apologised? And remembering the last time he had laughed at her—how could she ever face him again to so much as begin to apologise!

Kelsey spent another fitful night, her problems seeming insurmountable. For she still had the problem of trying to keep Serle and her father apart for the next month. And as trustworthy as she now knew Serle to be, she just couldn't face going to him with the only solution that presented itself—that of asking him to play along with her for the remainder of her father's time in Japan.

Sighing deeply as she got out of bed to start another nerve-tearing day, she saw that if the problems she had chewed over in her waking hours weren't enough, she just didn't have the first notion how she was going to repay Serle the twenty thousand pounds she had as good as stolen from him.

Somehow she got through the day with Yukiko popping in unexpectedly for nothing more than a chat, giving her tormented mind a breather. But her anxieties were back full force when her father, not long home, commented in a by-the-way fashion:

'I expect you and Serle will be married before too long.'

'Er—what makes you say that?' she asked, head down as she concentrated hard on the button she was sewing on one of his shirts, seeing that any notion she had of extending her 'tiff' with Serle until her father was safely back in England wasn't going to be swallowed.

'Common sense,' he replied, and not having any idea that his daughter had much more on her mind than she could handle, he smiled as he told her, 'With Serle having that big house up the road all to himself, it's only logical that you should move in with him when I go.' And unconsciously delivering the straw that broke the camel's back, 'The Company will want this house when I move out—it would be daft for you to look for somewhere else to live when I leave.'

With deliberate movements, Kelsey put down her sewing. 'Dad——' she began; it was on the tip of her tongue to tell him everything. It just hadn't occurred to her that she would have to leave the bungalow, and she just didn't think she could take something else going wrong. But when Henry Marchant looked up, with not a sign of depression about him, as there would be if she told him the whole of it and revealed how much further he was in debt, Kelsey just couldn't do it. 'I've got a headache,' she invented, when patiently he waited for her to finish. 'Would you mind if we had dinner late? I'd like to go for a walk to see if I can clear it.'

How long she stayed away from the bungalow trying to accept that this last blow was not, when compared with everything else, such a hammer blow, Kelsey had no idea. But dark had descended by the time she had herself in hand again and had decided that looking for fresh accommodation for the remainder of her stay after her father had left was something that would just have to be sorted out when he was safely in England. As would what sort of story she could concoct for when, unmarried, she arrived home shortly after him. For the moment she had more than enough to try and cope with.

Believing herself to be more composed, she turned into the short street where she lived. It was a hot night, and walking up the path to the house, she could easily see that her father had slid back the outer door to let as much air as could be found circulate through the entrance and small hall which were not air-conditioned.

But her composure was to go streaking the moment she raised her foot to step up from the entrance area and on to the hall floor. She *froze*, a short strangled sound leaving her—for her father was not alone! And simultaneously, or so it seemed, as she heard the clink of glasses that suggested he was offering their guest refreshment, she knew, as her father began to speak, exactly who their visitor was!

'Since you tell me you've done away with the go-between's services, Serle, might I guess that this personal—matter—that brings you here is that you've come yourself, in true British fashion, to ask for the hand of my daughter?'

Scarlet, gasping for air, Kelsey found she had hurried away from the house. 'Oh, my God!' she groaned out loud. She paced up and down outside her home. Serle must have walked over, she guessed, otherwise the sight of his car would have tipped her off. And had she not deliberately chosen to take her walk in an opposite direction from his house, she could well have bumped into him!

What was going on in there? What was Serle saying? Was he laughing his head off at her father's suggestion that he had come to formally ask for her hand?

Oh God, she thought, and knew she should go in and break it up. But she found she just did not yet have the courage.

How could she face the man who last night had roared with laughter at her heated challenge of did he want to marry her? How could she again face that laughter her father had brought on by his old-fashioned question?

For nail-chewing, hair-tearing minutes she tried to get herself under control. But when perhaps only ten minutes had elapsed, although it seemed like hours, it suddenly came through her highly agitated thoughts that her father might, right at this minute, be in the depths of despair if Serle had merely called to ask for the return of his twenty thousand pounds.

It was that thought that got her moving. With her heart hammering, Kelsey forced herself to approach the house. Then, as she turned up the path, again she froze. For ten minutes, it seemed, was all the time Serle Falconer had needed to flatten her father. For he was coming away from the house—and he had seen her!

Slowly Kelsey was released from her frozen immobility. But by then Serle was only a few yards from her. Taking off at a sprint, she would have dashed past him and into the house—only she didn't get the chance.

A hard hand on her arm was hauling her back mid-flight as she went to pass him without a word. Her cheeks scarlet again, there were no words in her either as she found herself being marched away from the path and round into the lamplit street, and backed against the high shrubbery.

Seeing she was making no move to get away, indeed Kelsey was now feeling too winded to think of escape, Serle let go her arm. And there in the diminished glow of a street lamp he revealed that, when she couldn't remember having made a sound, he had been aware of her arrival home the first time.

'How much did you hear?' was the first question he put to her, his voice even, level, which made her hope hers wasn't going to come out sounding as staccato as inside she felt.

'Not—very much,' she managed to answer. 'I think—I must have arrived on your heels.'

She had nothing more to add. But he was waiting for more. She sensed tension in him, and knew her nerves were shot to pieces that she should imagine he was tense in any way. It was she who was tense, embarrassment swamping her again as he waited still to have his answer to the question of how much she had heard.

'All I heard,' she said, made to go on by his very silence, but having to swallow as, hoping he had done with laughing, she brought out, 'was my father asking—if you'd come to—ask for my hand.'

'That was all you heard?' he demanded to know, and that tough note that entered his voice as he sought to find out if she was lying gave her, fortunately, sufficient mettle to snap:

'I didn't stay around to hear you tell him it was all some—some game you were playing for your own amusement!'

As swiftly as it had come, her flare of anger died. She wouldn't look at him, but she saw him move back on his heels, as slowly he drawled:

'Rather a pricey game, wouldn't you say?'

And she had thought she had done away with anger! In no position to let fly, just his couldn't-care-less tone, apart from what he said, had the turmoil in her that had been looking for an outlet blasting its way to the surface. And Kelsey left her launching pad.

'So that *was* your reason for coming!' she rocketed, in orbit without needing to think about it, red the only colour she could see, her fury at what he had done to her father sending tension and embarrassment scattering, her eruption instant and furious. 'You came to ask for your money back!' And, having been ripped apart all day by her thoughts, she had suddenly come to life as, too angry all at once to let him get a word in, she did look at him as he was about to interrupt. 'Well, I hope you're satisfied, Falconer. I hope it makes you feel good inside that you've just finished off my father!'

'Finished off . . .'

Kelsey still wasn't in any mood to let him interrupt. 'Yes, finished off,' she stormed on. 'You've just taken away the very last hope he had of getting back to England, of getting to my mother!'

'How have I done that?'

'*How?* You know damn well how!' she hissed, not liking at all his cool, reasonable-sounding tone when she was so flaming mad. 'You *knew* I'd give him that money,' she charged, trembling with temper, her own hopes that her ideally suited parents would be reunited now in ashes. 'Just as you knew he would straight away purchase an air ticket and settle with his creditors, making him more in debt than he was before. You know him well enough to know that he won't leave Japan now—not now you've told him that money was never intended as a—gift to me.'

She could feel her anger draining away, and knew she had the thought of her parent thinking the money was a bridal gift to thank for that. But her anger spurted again when she saw his hand come out as though to take hold of her.

'Don't you touch me ever again!' she flared, fiercely knocking his hand away. In the lamplight, she saw his expression turn hostile, his features a chiselled mask. And knowing the weakness he could wreak in her, she was having to make herself remember how her father had trusted him—and look where it had got him! She felt real fury again as she spurned, 'My God, I was right not to trust you!' And believing it for those few seconds, 'Not only do I not trust you, you swine, I hate, loathe and detest you!' she reviled him. Furious still, she would have gone streaking away from him, had not cruel biting fingers snaked to her arm and jerked her back to face him.

It was a mistake to look into his face. For grim though his expression was, coldly furious as his face was, just the erect taut stance of him telling her that nobody called Serle Falconer names and got away with it, she knew what a pathetic lie it had been to say that she hated him. But loving him as she did, Kelsey was made of sterner stuff than to wilt because it looked as though, having let her get all her days and nights of impotent searching for a way out released from her system, the culmination being the big bang of her fiery explosion, she still wasn't going to be flattened without a fight.

'Want more?' she scorned snappily, refusing to let him see his hold on her was hurting.

'I've heard more than enough,' he returned icily. 'But just to keep the record straight,'—oh, how he loved everything straight, didn't he, this man her father had called highly principled—'the subject of money was never under discussion in my talk with your father.'

Her reaction was immediate, and open-mouthed. 'Never discussed?' She didn't believe him. That twenty thousand *must* have had a mention. 'I don't believe y . . .' she stopped, the sudden increased pressure on her arm cutting off the blood supply to her hand as she saw that he didn't take it very kindly that on top of all she had hurled, she was now calling him a liar.

'What was under discussion,' he told her grittily, and not at all charmingly, 'was our marriage.'

'Our—marriage!' Her heart suddenly thundering, her legs threatening to fold, Kelsey sifted her stunned brain and found a choky, 'But—but we aren't going to—be married.'

His reply, as charmless as before, had her swallowing and trying to get her head to wake up as she saw only the contradiction of what he said, in relation to him throwing her arm away from him as though it offended him to touch her.

'I want you,' he told her shortly, and only then did she perceive that where her temper had been red-hot when she had gone for him, his anger, more controlled, had been quietly simmering. Only then did she see that Serle Falconer was now in a positively seething rage. 'And I'll have you,' he bit in a tone there was no arguing with. And his voice was then ice cold, sending a shiver down her spine, 'But by *God*,' he vowed, 'you'll *crawl to me first* before I take you!'

As those vehemently cutting words hit her ears, so Kelsey saw then, how dreadfully she had insulted him by her heated talk of loathing him, of not trusting, of calling him a liar. When she had full past experience of Serle not taking insults from the likes of her without squaring up accounts—she had done it again!

But marriage! Was he meaning to make her pay—this time by making her marry him—this man she had told not five minutes ago that he was hated by her? Even he wouldn't go that far to get redress for an insult, would he?

Kelsey found herself in more confusion. For loving him there was nothing more she wanted than to marry him—But against that was the ideal she had set herself—and how could marriage to this man, who looked now as though hitting her would be preferable to bedding her, turn out to be anything like the sort of marriage she had always dreamt of for herself?

That Serle was silently watching, waiting for her answer, told her he was confident she had no answer for him but to agree. He wasn't pressing her, was he? But then, he had no need to! He knew, she thought, her anger against him not done with yet as her independent streak broke cover, that if she said no, her father would not be making his eagerly looked forward trip to England.

'So it does all boil down to the money,' she said at last—making herself go on when his eyes narrowed as though seeing another insult coming his way. 'What you're really saying is that you want my body and that you're prepared to pay for it.'

She heard his sharp intake of breath—saw that his hands were clenched. And for one terrified moment as the light caught his jutting jaw and showed a fierce glitter in his eyes, Kelsey was sure he was going to resort to physical violence and not content himself with just looking as though to slap her would give him no small pleasure.

But when a few taut seconds had passed and she did not feel the sting of his hand across her face, all fear of him, and every other emotion in her, subsided. Every other emotion that was except hurt. And it was that hurt, when Serle had never pretended to love her, yet confessed to wanting her, that had her goading when common sense would have told her, since she had no option, that she should just quietly agree and not risk the snapping of that tight control he was exercising:

'You've said you want me, Serle, but surely in this day and age you're not thinking you have to marry me to get what you want?'

The hurt in her was growing, egging her on when she could see his control was on the point of fracturing. And, flippant outside to hide that she was breaking up inside, she even managed a light laugh as she tossed airily at his silent watchful figure:

'For a sum like twenty thousand, you don't have to marry me to get me to *crawl!*'

His fury broke. But he did not hit her. Kelsey wondered if it would have been better if he had—that pain might ease the pain that was going on inside.

'Damn and blast you Kelsey Marchant!' he threw in a seething, furious undertone. 'To hell with the money! And to hell with you and your propositioning me! You'll come to me, and I'll have you—but on my terms.'

'Wh-what terms?' she dared to ask, flinching back from the violence she saw in him.

'You will *give* yourself—I'm not paying,' he roared, gone was his control on his temper. 'For a start you are going to marry me as soon as I can arrange it.'

'But . . .' she tried to intercept.

'But,' he ignored her, 'I shall only make you my wife when you come to me voluntarily.' And if she hadn't understood that, 'I'll have none of the "lie back and think of England" nonsense. When you come to me, it will be because you want me as much as I want you.'

Kelsey wasn't defeated yet. 'And money doesn't come into it!' she scoffed, trying to let him know that she wouldn't marry him unless she was forced to—she had pride too—it would just about sink her if he ever suspected that she loved him.

Serle took a pace back from her—and she guessed he had recaptured his lost temper that her ears weren't singing for her jibing. But there was a threat in voice there was no mistaking when he gave her her answer.

'Only so far that if you don't marry me,' he replied, a silky edge coming to make his threat sound even more ominous, 'I have it in my power to see to it that your parents never get that chance to get together again.'

CHAPTER NINE

WITH her independent spirit outraged to be forced to marry Serle Falconer, her years of dreaming of the ideal marriage she would have gone for ever, it was an outwardly smiling Kelsey who went through a simple marriage ceremony with Serle Falconer three weeks later.

Without knowing quite how, she had kept a smile pinned to her face throughout the sham of the celebratory meal, and knew as the meal drew to a close that she had convinced her father and Yukiko, their two witnesses, that she was every bit as happy as she was meant to be.

But now, with the meal at an end, her glance caught that of the man she had married, and momentarily, as the hatred she had drummed up against him took the smile from her face, Kelsey knew that he was one person who had seen through her phoney smile. Their eyes steady on each other, war being declared in hers, his sending back a mocking 'I should care!' she knew that he hadn't been fooled for a minute by her too ready laugh at any quip her father made.

'Ready, my dear?'

How she hated that 'my dear'! Kelsey stood up, her smile back in place as she turned to her father, who was going to drive Yukiko home.

'I'll be at the airport to see you off on Saturday,' she told him, wishing with all her heart that she was going with him.

'We'll both be there,' chipped in Serle, making her father beam that Serle was making it sound as though he couldn't bear to let her out of his sight, when Kelsey knew he would only be accompanying her to see that she didn't get on that plane too.

Want her he might, she thought mutinously, as she sat beside him in the car being driven to her new home, but he wasn't trusting her an inch. He wasn't so slow that he hadn't already figured out that as his wife she could claim half of everything he owned, and with his wealth, the twenty thousand he had given her was a mere nothing if she absconded and he tried to take her to court over it.

Not that she would abscond, she had more honour than he credited her with. Married to him, the deed done, Kelsey knew it was, for her, a commitment for life. Though what sort of a life it would be, heaven alone knew, because while Serle might want her, if he was waiting for her to crawl to him before he took her, then wouldn't he have a long wait!

'Are you going to sulk for the rest of the day?'

Serle's short-and-to-the-point question brought Kelsey away from her mutinous thoughts. 'Of course not, *my dear*,' she replied acidly. And not liking to think that her sarcasm had amused him, she dug in further to knock the grin of his face, 'As soon as I'm out of this car and where you aren't, I'm positive I shall return to being my old sweet self!'

She felt better suddenly to have scored a few points; he wasn't smiling any longer, anyway. And that grunt she received was a fair indication that his wedding day wasn't all he might have wished for either.

Thank goodness he'd had the sense to do without a honeymoon, she thought, as the car stopped outside the house she had not stepped foot in again since that night she had rushed from it covered in mortification that she had asked him if he wanted to marry her.

Tears pricked her eyes as the love she felt for him tried to get past the barrier of hatred she had erected.

'What's this?'

She hadn't been quick enough to get out of the car,

and she was back to hating Serle, who had come round to her side. Trust him to notice the glisten of unshed tears in her eyes, she thought, angry with herself for being so weak, angry with him for being so observant.

'All brides weep on their wedding day, didn't you know?' she replied flippantly, and stepping out of the car, she just couldn't resist another squirt of acid. 'With joy,' she added with heavily laced sarcasm.

She had expected a soured grunt but, for her pains, received a laugh that didn't endear him to her at all.

'Poor little Kelsey,' he said softly, and she could have knocked his legs from under him at the underlying mockery there. 'You are the romantic I once called you, aren't you?'

'I don't know what you're talking about,' she snapped, and would have walked past him had he not halted her by the simple expedient of taking hold of her by her chin and tilting her face so she had to look at him.

'You'd dreamed of orange blossom, with birds singing in the trees. A proposal in the moonlight, with . . .'

'With the chance to say no, if I wanted to,' she retorted hotly, then saw the gleam of humour in his eyes that without too much effort he had got her away from the coldly sarcastic female she had become these last three weeks. Kelsey wrenched herself away and marched to the front door.

At a more leisurely pace, he followed, deliberately keeping her waiting, she thought, since she couldn't go in until he came and opened up.

'And since I'm going to have to live here, I'd like my own front door key,' she snapped, the acid returning.

'How about a key to your bedroom door?' Serle came back.

The door open, Kelsey flounced in. 'I thought I was the one who had to do the crawling,' she threw over her shoulder, realising strangely, that contrary to what she had told him, she did trust him and did not have one single qualm that he might take it into his head to take her against her will.

'Crawling was perhaps the wrong word to use,' said Serle when, because she wanted to go to her room and as yet had no idea which one he had allocated to her, she had stopped where she stood.

But as what he said made her heart pound, and made her spin round, as the thought occurred that she might be wrong to trust him, she just had to ask, her eyes going wide:

'Wh-what do you mean?'

As he observed the sudden panic in her eyes, his expression suddenly hardened. 'Obviously not what you're thinking,' he said grimly—and turning her about with a none too gentle hand, 'I'll show you to your room—your private room.'

Her heart steadying, Kelsey began to climb the stairs with him. They had reached the landing before Serle spoke again, and his voice was as terse as it had been before when, stopping at one of the doors before leading on, bluntly he told her:

'This is my room.' Silently, solemnly Kelsey looked at him. 'This is where you will come when you're ready.'

And that will be never, she thought when minutes later, having shown her to the room that was to be hers, the cases she had packed and given him standing in the centre of the carpet, he had left her to it.

Her unpacking did not take all that long, though with a few hours to go before she could plead tiredness and climb into bed, Kelsey found that having thought she would be glad to see the back of him, her treacherous heart had her wanting to be in his company.

What for? she made herself ask. For, before he had witnessed her panic at the thought that he might force her into bed with him he had treated her for the most part lightly—as if he had understood her sadness that her ideals of what her marriage should be were so different from the reality of what it was—but he had since that moment been terse and cold with her.

A romantic, he had called her, she recalled, and went over to where a bouquet of roses had been placed on the dressing table. Tears filled her eyes again, as accepting that the gesture could well have been his quaint sarcasm at work—he had come calling that first day with mocking roses in his hand—it could equally well have been that he was trying to put some of the romance he thought her soul craved into a day that should have been romance-filled.

Two weeks later, her father now back in England, Kelsey knew it had been Serle's quaint brand of sarcasm at work when he had placed those roses in her room. He hadn't got a streak of romanticism in him, she thought, trying to get cross about it, but finding that two weeks of living in the same house with him had weakened her rebellion and left only sadness there that he would never love her.

On the surface polite, his sarcasm could be cutting when occasionally in that first week some perversity made her try to needle him. Or was it perversity? Having admitted that her hatred of being forced into marriage was a weak emotion compared to the all-consuming love she had for him, she had to think then, was it not perversity, but that she wanted to prick him into noticing her as a person and not as another piece of furniture he came home to each night?

Perhaps that was a little unfair, she mused. For, cool with her as Serle was, he usually asked how her day had gone. And several times in these last two weeks he had taken the trouble to take her out to places he thought might amuse her. Though he had made no mention of any plan to take her anywhere tonight, so sighing deeply, Kelsey took her mind off the sadness of her thoughts, and put her mind to what sort of meal she should prepare.

'What have you done with yourself today?' Serle

asked pleasantly, having politely complimented her on the *marchand de vin* she had laboured over to get the sauce just right.

This evening was one of the few stay-at-home evenings when Serle hadn't found his work in his study more appealing than spending more than a few after-dinner minutes with her. If only some feeling of companionship was there, Kelsey found herself thinking, then maybe their marriage might have a chance to get off the ground.

'Oh, this and that,' she shrugged from her chair opposite him in the sitting room. And feeling stilted by their lack of companionship, 'Yukiko rang and we went into town.' And hastily, 'Mrs Kaido, as you know, takes care of the housework.'

'Good God, you don't have to make excuses for not being here every hour of the day!' came shooting from Serle.

'Perhaps you would rather I wasn't here at all,' she flared. 'Perhaps . . .' she stopped. Oh, dear heaven, so much for her thinking, when he hadn't departed for his study, that there might be a chance for something to grow!

'If you're hinting at divorce,' he said darkly, getting to his feet, 'forget it.'

'No chance?' Her pride made her put it as a question.

Serle favoured her with one of those grim looks she was getting used to. 'Not one in a million.'

'Fight the good fight, eh?' she questioned, and thought he was going to flatten her, until his sense of humour won through.

'I'd sooner be in the ring with you than anyone,' he said drolly, but she didn't miss his grin, and it heartened her.

'Steady, Serle,' she mocked, 'that was nearly a compliment!'

Guessing, since he had not resumed his seat, that he

had decided to work in his study after all, she got up, in an endeavour to be first to leave the room.

She had drawn level with him when Serle's voice made her halt. 'I haven't complimented you very much, have I?'

She turned to face him, her heart suddenly pounding to see that there was none of the coldness she had witnessed in his eyes for her so many times.

'I'm not – interested in insincere compliments,' she said, her voice grown a little husky.

'I wouldn't dream of offering insincere compliments,' he said, a smile lurking at the corners of his mouth. 'But you do have hidden talents, Kelsey.'

'I can cook,' she said her feet refusing to move from the spot when Serle took that step that brought him right up close to her.

'You can cook,' he agreed. That smile broke softly as he ran a finger down her nose. 'I never realised what culinary delights I was letting myself in for when I married you.'

'I—er—like cooking,' was all she was able to get out, his touch, just that one finger on her nose, drifting down to the corner of her mouth, setting off a weakness in her. She cleared her throat. 'I used to cook for Gran before . . .'

'And you're beautiful too,' Serle interrupted softly. 'Did anyone ever tell you that?'

Just one hand to her face, and Kelsey felt as if she were being seduced. Was that what it was? Was Serle trying to make it easier for her to go to him? 'Er—they—might have done,' she said, barely remembering what the question was, let alone who, if anybody, had told her that she was beautiful—and then she thought that maybe all she had to do was kiss Serle. Maybe he wasn't expecting her to visit him in his bedroom, maybe—maybe, if she kissed him—he would take her to his room.

'Serle,' she said his chokily.

He did not move away when she had nothing to add, but was waiting, a sudden fire lighting his eyes. I should kiss him, she thought. One tiny step forward that was all that was needed for body contact. He was waiting for her to kiss him, she knew it, just as clearly as she could read that look in his eyes that said, 'Come to me.'

She opened her mouth, she wanted him, wanted to tell him that she wanted him. But before the words could leave her, quite without warning, unexpectedly, and never thought of, suddenly Kelsey found that she was in the grip of the most overwhelming and hopeless shyness she had never experienced.

Drowning in a vortex she was unable to surface from, she was then trying to force out other words. Other words to say, 'Help me—I've never been with a man before.' But gripped as she was, shyness having a strangle-hold on her, those words would not leave her either.

She saw traces of puzzlement enter his eyes, but she knew he could not be expected to translate what her eyes were asking him to understand, since she had given him the clear impression that she'd had several lovers.

Then it was too late for her to find the words to ask for his help. For his hand had fallen from her face. But he still stood facing her; not moving when she wanted that hand, that arm around her—anything, anything to help her with this unutterable shyness that had come from nowhere to take charge of her.

But that arm did not come around her. And though that 'Come to me' message was back in his eyes, Kelsey knew then, as highly principled as her father had said he was, that Serle having stated that he would only take her when she did go to him, he was not going to make that first move.

She saw the corners of his mouth start to pick up in what could have been a smile of encouragement. But suddenly, bogged down by unthought of modesty as she was, Kelsey found her nerves were getting to her. She knew a deal about Serle, but there was a deal she did not know about him. Suppose, she thought, doubt merging with that dreadful shyness, suppose that all along Serle, a master at deviousness, didn't want her at all! Suppose those signals she thought she was reading in his eyes were not the signals she thought they were!

Having been spellbound, fastened to the spot for countless seconds; having stood rooted, locked, silent, while trying to read his eyes, she had the mortifying thought—was Serle only drawing her on, encouraging her, in order to—reject her?

That humiliating thought was enough to have her dropping her eyes from the hypnotic hold of his. And, the spell broken, Kelsey would not look at him again.

'I'm going to bed,' she mumbled. And with ragged finality, 'Goodnight,' she said, and she was in no mind then to hang around for his answer.

She had her answer, though, when up in her room, still trembling from the encounter, she heard his frustration being eased as the study door was crashed shut with an angry slam. Though whether his frustration stemmed from the fact that for a third time he had been near to taking her, and hadn't, or whether it was from the frustration of not being able to tell her 'No, thanks' when she offered herself, Kelsey was still too mixed up to be able to fathom. She did not sleep well that night.

Reasoning that he had been able to cook his own breakfast before she had moved in, Kelsey stayed in her bedroom until she heard Serle leave for work. That he had not come to her door to ask was she all right, or to tell her he was off, was sufficient for her to know that beautiful, though he might have called her, he wasn't pining for sight of her that morning.

Nor was he pining for a sight of her when he came home that night, for no sooner had his meal been eaten than he had shut himself away in his study. And by the time another couple of days had passed with Serle being on the surface polite, but with a coolness seeming to be growing in him towards her, Kelsey was owning to herself that she was very definitely beginning to find his coldness irksome.

It did no good to remember the fire she had seen in his eyes for her the other night, for as another couple of days passed, with a remoteness about Serle she found disconcerting, Kelsey was well on the way to believing she had imagined that fire.

Pride made her pretend that she didn't care a tinker's cuss that their meal times together, about the only times she saw him these days, were spent with barely monosyllabic conversation between them. But Serle's withdrawal from her made her face the fact that even though he was often sarcastic, she missed the warmth of his conversation.

By the time a week had passed with them living like strangers in the same house, a state of affairs she would have welcomed on her wedding day, Kelsey admitted she had no more pseudo-hatred in her heart for him.

With that word hatred in her mind, she was back to recalling how she had told Serle that she hated him that night he had bluntly said, 'I want you.'

Want her! It looked like it, she thought, as his key in the door told her he had returned home from his office. She made no move to go and greet him, but then she never had done, but stayed in the sitting room thinking he knew where to find her if he wanted her.

That word 'want' again! she thought dismissively—then found that the word wouldn't be dismissed. But it was when she discovered that she was teaming that word 'want' with the word 'hate', and following on, the memory of her telling Serle that she only ever went to bed with men whom she was fond of, that sirens started to sound inside her.

No, she thought, trying not to get excited at this new and latest thought that had come and would not be ignored. It couldn't be—could it? And she was then trying to stay calm as she analysed that what with Serle being the very high-principled person that he was, could it be that he—didn't want to take her while he thought that she hated him! Was he, in fact, biding his time hoping that by living in the same house she might learn to grow fond of him!

Rot, said her common sense. Serle had gone round like a bear with a sore head all week, barely talking to her unless he had to. Was that the action of a man who wanted her affection? And anyway, came cold icy logic she didn't want, to suppose that Serle wanted her affection had to mean that he was just a teeny bit fond of her, didn't it? As she thought of the cold way he had been with her all week, her theory was knocked firmly on the head.

Though that didn't stop those same thoughts from returning when later at a dinner she sat opposite him. He works too hard, he looks tired, she thought—and went on to thinking that not once this week had he asked if she had had a good day. Unhappily she realised how much she missed his ordinary enquiry, then found suddenly that she was thinking that if he wanted to remain a taciturn brute, then, as his marriage partner, she had certain rights. That he had certain rights too, but seemed to have gone off the idea of claiming them, was starting to niggle her, she had to own.

'I've had a good day today,' she found herself blurting out à propos nothing. Strung up within herself, she refused to feel a fool that he looked down the length of the table at her as though to say, 'Bully for you!'

'I'm pleased to hear it,' he said suavely, but didn't, she noticed, bother to ask what she had done—which, while she realised it was just as well since she had done nothing out of the ordinary, annoyed her just the same.

Irritably she pushed her coffee cup away from her. In a moment Serle would stand up and politely ask her to excuse him as he had work to do. She wondered what he would say if she said no, she wouldn't excuse him.

Probably give her one of those hard staring looks and say 'Too bad' and go just the same.

Rebelliously, Kelsey stared at the wedding ring on her hand. A fine marriage this is! she fumed, and heard the scrape of his chair. And from nowhere came the words, 'Just for the record, Falconer—I don't hate you.' Oh God, she thought as soon as the words were out, was she mad? Where was her pride?

It was pride that made her tilt her chin defiantly to look at him. Her words had stayed him from going anywhere, she saw, as she was made to suffer his long and inscrutable stare.

Then softly, his eyes never leaving her face, though not revealing a thing of his thoughts, he drawled slowly:

'I didn't think you did.'

Swine! she thought, her reasoning that that was why he hadn't taken her just so much wishful thinking. Well, if he was waiting for her to tell him she was fond of him, he could go on waiting! But as the terrifying thought came that maybe, just as he had known that she didn't hate him, he likewise knew that she was in love with him, Kelsey, since Serle was waiting for what other gem she had to impart, was left to fall back on heavy sarcasm, which soon took the look of interest from his face.

'Just thought I'd mention it,' she remarked casually. 'I can see you've been losing sleep over something.'

'Not over you, my dear,' was slammed back at her stingingly, 'Never think that.'

In bed that night, it did no good to know that all he ever thought about was work—that it was work he was losing sleep over. Kelsey gave way to weak tears. He wants me out, she thought, dabbing at her eyes. But having kicked all the way against marrying him, having come to live with him, she knew, however unbearable living with him was, it was preferable to living without him—that she didn't want to go.

Her sleep that night was of the patchy variety. She

woke again about three in the morning, and alarm rocketed through her all at once. Her first thought as the room seemed to tilt was that she was about to faint. Then when she didn't black out but definitely felt the room move, the word 'earthquake' shot into her head.

In a flash she was streaking for the door, Serle her only thought. She must get to him! Her first grab, in her panic for the door handle, missed it. But she got the door open in her next attempt, and was out on the landing to see Serle, a robe hastily thrown round him, coming towards her.

'It's all right,' were his first reassuring words, and the fact that his cold tone had gone was of more comfort than words.

'Is it an earthquake?' she asked fearfully, and felt more comforted when he placed an arm around her trembling shoulders.

'We'd have known about it for sure by now if it was,' he said easily, turning her to the head of the stairs. 'More likely a small earth tremor, but we'll go downstairs for a while, I think.'

He's worried, Kelsey thought, as with his arm still about her, together they descended the stairs. Although his voice is calm, he's worried. The tremor, if that was what it was, had woken him too, so unless he was already awake as she had been, it must have been a big one, not the small one he had suggested.

With the comment, 'Fancy a cup of tea?' Serle led her into the kitchen.

'I—wouldn't mind,' she replied, her mind going off at a tangent to wonder if he should be using electrical appliances such as the kettle in the circumstances. Perhaps he's taking the risk to reassure me that there's nothing to worry about, she thought, her initial panic subsiding, but her insides churning.

Serle sat her down at the kitchen table and removed his arm. Straight away Kelsey wanted his arm back. And she couldn't restrain a shiver as Serle, having filled the kettle and switched on, turning from the kitchen unit.

'Cold?' he inquired, when it was a warm night, his eyes flicking over the look of her in her short cotton nightdress. 'I'd offer you this,' he said, plucking at his robe with a couple of fingers, and a most charming grin coming out, 'only I ain't decent underneath!'

Kelsey managed a light laugh, though she couldn't help seeing the faint puzzlement in his eyes that she, a girl who slept around occasionally, should blush to know that he hadn't a stitch on underneath.

'I'm—not cold,' she got out, feeling suddenly hot all over to realise, when it hadn't dawned on her before, that she had been too panic-stricken to think of snatching up her robe in transit.

Casually, as he placed a cup of tea in front of her, Kelsey crossed her arms over her breasts, aware as she was that the dark tips of them must show through the near-transparent cotton she had on.

Serle brought his tea to the table too. Feeling suddenly tense, Kelsey searched for something to say, and found it in the apology that was long overdue to him.

'I never did get round to saying sorry for all those dreadful things I accused you of—those dreadful things I said to you that night . . .'

'That night I asked you to marry me?' he filled in for her when her voice faltered.

As she remembered it, there hadn't been much asking about it. But suddenly, as tension emptied out of her, for the first time she felt a sense of real companionship with him. Whether it was just because he had seen her panic and had lost that coldness as he'd tried to reassure her that it wasn't an earthquake, she didn't know. But all at once, she had lost her loneliness of spirit, and it just wasn't important any longer that she had been pressganged into marrying him.

'That's right,' she replied. 'I meant to apologise before, only . . .'

'Only we never stopped fighting long enough?' he suggested, with a charm, a warmth about his mouth that made her feel she could tell him anything just then.

'Something like that,' she agreed. 'Though I honestly did believe at one stage that you'd persuaded my father to invest in a scheme which you knew full well to be worthless.'

Feeling not the least disloyal to her father now, realising as she was only then that Serle had the first call on her loyalty, Kelsey explained the circumstances she had found her father in when she had first come to Japan. Telling him that, knowing her father to be a cautious man, only underlined everything he had said as being true, even if the worse for drink when he had told her.

'I didn't get to know the real truth of the matter, that led by him, my own interpretation was widely off course, until after I'd given him the money you sent with Mr Saito,' she ended.

'But instead of apologising, you lost your temper and told me that not only did you hate, but that you didn't trust me either?' put in Serle.

'You—know I don't hate you,' she said, and daring a look at him, saw that his eyes were holding a warm look for her. She swallowed as his gaze travelled to where, while relating all her father had said that first day, she had forgotten to keep her arms in front of her. 'Just,' she said, having sudden difficulty in breathing as her breasts seemed to hold some fascination for him, 'just as you know I trust you.'

Her telling him that she trusted him, caused him to drag his eyes back from the darkened areas thrusting at her nightdress.

'You—trust me?' he asked, and she wondered if that was a thread of hoarseness she heard in his voice, as if—he was doubting himself his own trustworthiness.

'Yes—yes, I do,' she replied, fighting against a need to fold her arms across her again.

But she soon saw that she had no need to feel shy, or to feel in any way that it was in Serle's mind to remove that outer covering from her. For all at once his chair was grating back from the table, and he was saying:

'It's over half an hour since that first tremor—I'm sure it's safe for you to go back to your bed.'

Confusion hit her that she couldn't have read what she had thought she had read in his eyes—that she had misread that look that she'd thought said he still wanted her. And Kelsey left her chair and was at the kitchen door before her confusion cleared sufficiently for her to wonder, was Serle sending her to her chaste little bed alone, because, because she had told him that she trusted him? Did he want her—but was that word 'trust' now getting in the way? Confused again, she went to open the kitchen door. But something was stopping her from making that final action to leave.

Courage she had never thought to have, pushed on by the despairing feeling that never might she ever be as close again to Serle as she had felt this last half hour, made her say:

'Can—can I come to—your bed?'

Her back to him, she refused to wilt as the brazen words she had spoken bounced back to her ears. Then silence greeted her—a silence that went on too long and had her face burning, so that she was glad he could not see it. Then his voice came, terse, all friendliness gone.

'Because you're afraid there might be another tremor?'

Kelsey wanted to leave then, but still that same something from before was keeping her prisoner. 'Because I—want to,' she said, and yearning, she waited, wanting with all her heart to feel his two arms come round her.

But Serle's arms did not come round her. Kelsey did

not hear him make so much as a step towards her. 'It's taken an earth tremor to make you realise that, has it?'

She didn't want him analysing her reasons. Didn't want to hear that note in his voice that said he did not believe she wanted to be in his bed for any other reason than that she was scared stiff that the building might shake again. Why she didn't just open that door and leave then, she didn't know. Though vaguely she was aware of something trying to get through the confusion to the effect that if they were ever to make anything of their marriage then there had to be some giving on her part.

'I've known for—some time now,' she forced out, 'that I—want you, Serle.' She heard his short intake of breath, and tried to go on. 'But—but . . .'

'Don't stop now.'

Was he being sarcastic? Aware her ears were ready to pick up every nuance, even those that weren't there, Kelsey made herself turn and face him, hoping, if her ears were playing her false, that she might read more from the expression on his face.

But his look was shuttered, his eyes telling her nothing, as he insisted, 'But—what?'

'But—I wasn't sure about you.'

That shuttered look went taut, as he rapped, 'Don't lie! Not at this—fascinating stage.'

'I'm not lying!' The words left her hotly, pride there, shame there that she had offered herself and looked like being rejected as she had once thought. 'I . . .'

'You know damn well I want you,' he cut through her roughly, sounding not in the least lover-like, to her mind.

'You've got a very peculiar way of showing it,' she snapped.

'I could take you any time I care to, and you damn well know I could,' he started to fire back, and she recognised the truth of that remark from the two occasions she had been in his arms. Then abruptly he was checking his temper, and appeared to be giving the consideration she wanted to her comment that he had a peculiar way of showing that he still wanted her. 'Okay, so maybe I haven't been going around tearing your clothes from you,' he said thoughtfully, and paused then, before he said, 'So if I'm to believe you, that it isn't just that you're frightened to sleep alone for fear of another tremor—why not let it all out and tell me why you haven't said anything about wanting me before this?'

Nerves, fear that he would laugh at her if she told him she had discovered a shyness in her, fear that he would roar his head off if she told him that she was a virgin, made Kelsey stiffen.

'You'll—laugh at me,' she tossed at him angrily. 'You're good at doing that.'

His look was mocking. 'I could do with a laugh,' he tossed back. And, his expression going harsh, 'If memory serves, I haven't had a good laugh in all the short time we've been married.'

And to Kelsey, that was it. She had offered, he had dissected. But to give herself to someone for the first time, and to have that someone hardly able to kiss her for laughing, was more than flesh and blood could stand. Without needing to think about it, she turned to the door and threw it open. He wanted a good laugh, did he—well, let him laugh this off in his frustration!

'Go to hell, Falconer!' she yelled, and was through the door and was storming up to her room—but no laugh followed her.

CHAPTER TEN

IT was one thing to go charging up to her room, and quite another to find rest, Kelsey found. But it was not fear of another earth tremor that kept her pacing the floor—for in truth there was no room in her head for anything save thoughts of Serle and their farce of a marriage.

Farce was the right word for it, she thought, not attempting to get into bed, her thoughts too mutinous, the scene she had just raced from too vivid in her mind. Yet what was to be done about it? She didn't want a divorce, no matter how angry she was with him, no matter how many times she mentally called him a swine—and if Serle was to be believed, he didn't want a divorce either.

For several minutes Kelsey fumed over her marriage that wasn't a marriage. Then she thought of her parents' marriage and how happy they had always been in their married life, and were again now.

She sighed, her anger departing, and with her anger gone, she found then that her thinking was stretching further than it had ever been before. Found that she was pushing on to wonder, had her parents' marriage been blissful from the word go? Or had they had to work at it?

And then, quite suddenly, she realised that happy marriages didn't just happen overnight! That marriages *had* to be worked at before they could be called successful.

That it would be uphill work all the way if she endeavoured to work on the little she and Serle had going for them must be the understatement of the year, not to say a daunting idea. But, knowing all at once that she had grown up a lot since coming to Japan, Kelsey saw that she did not want a carbon copy of her parents' marriage; that her parents' marriage was special to them, and that she—she wanted a marriage that was special to her—and Serle.

For long moments she thought of the gigantic task it would be if she tried to make something special of her marriage where love lay only on the one side—hers. Did she want to try? She knew the answer to that without thinking about it. Just as she knew that she and Serle would never have a chance of resolving their differences while she was holding back on getting their marriage started; until she had made a start on resolving those differences and began acting—like a wife!

A trembling started inside her as she faced that she just didn't have the nerve to go along the landing and go through that bedroom door he had shown her as he had told her 'This is where you'll come when you're ready.'

Her eyes went to her chaste, lonely single bed. A bed that shouted at her that she would never be the wife she wanted to be to Serle, never have any sort of a marriage at all while she refused to take those few short steps along the landing it now seemed that Serle was insisting on.

And suddenly she was angry again. Angry with Serle for making her go to him. Angry with herself and her fear of taking those steps. So what if he laughed at her? So what if he rejected her? One thing was for sure, she couldn't go on like this for very much longer. Not giving herself time to think further Kelsey had left her room knowing if she didn't go now, she would never go.

But on reaching that all-important door, the thin line of light showing that he was not yet asleep, nerves attacked that alerted by the sound of his door opening, Serle would be watching her as she went through it.

'I should have put my robe on,' she thought

agitatedly. That thought followed by the trepidatious one of—I can't do it. Then she was forcing anger in that having made it this far she was getting cold feet.

And she was glad of that anger. Glad of the thought of, he's seen me in my nightie before. She had her hand on the door handle, and was turning it before cold feet could attack again.

Anger was her ally again when in the second of securing the door behind her, she saw that Serle, sitting four-square in the middle of the bed, having seen her, was observing her with a totally cool expression when with just the sight of his naked broad manly chest above the covers, she had never been in such a lather.

Swiftly, more to get her shape out of the light than anything, for she guessed that her nightdress was revealing too much, she marched over to where he half sat, half lay. If he said just one sarcastic word to the effect of 'What do I owe for the privilege of your visit?' then she knew she was going to hit him.

But Serle was saying nothing. Though he wasn't taking his eyes off her either. And desperately striving for words, any thought of repeating the 'I want you' which he demanded, went scattering from Kelsey. What she did find to say was an angry:

'Do you want *all* that bed?'

Not a glimmer of a smile or a welcome about him, she saw him obligingly move to allow her some space beside him. And instantly her nerves knotted together. Hesitating, when it was too late for hesitation.

But obliging still, and in invitation, Serle was pulling back the covers on the side he presumed she was intending to occupy. It was an invitation Kelsey needed.

The thin covers felt cold to her skin on such a warm night, as she too sat waiting for him to carry on from where his invitation had begun. But when, tense seconds ticking away with Serle not attempting to touch her, Kelsey was left staring and was back to wanting to thump him, as with his voice cool, like his expression, he asked:

'What next?'

'You tell me,' she flared. And when he wasn't telling her anything, but just propped himself up against the headboard, anger spurted again. It was that anger, anger mixed with nerves, that had her revealing that which in her anxious state she knew would have him roaring with laughter. 'I've never done this sort of thing before,' she snapped.

'Interesting,' Serle remarked, his eyes gone chilly. 'Though you can spare me the details of where you usually do "do this sort of thing"—that is,' he said laconically, 'if my instincts are right about what you are here *to do*.'

Insufferable devil! Kelsey fumed, anger fighting with jumping nerves that he hadn't understood what she was telling him, that he seemed more annoyed at the thought of the sordid little affairs she was telling him of than listening to what she was trying to tell him.

'If you laugh at me,' she said heatedly, when there didn't look to be a laugh in him, 'I swear I'll hit you!'

'Who's laughing?' he asked stonily.

'Well, shut up and—and *listen*,' she snapped. And she was in a lather again as she sought for the right words. 'I lied to you,' she managed after a moment. 'I—there haven't been any—er—other men.'

'I'm not with you,' was the reply she got for her trouble.

'Oh, for God's sake!' Kelsey exploded, at the end of her tether, ignoring the fact that his eyes were narrowing at her tone. 'You asked "What next?" I'm trying to tell you that I don't know—"what next" because I've never . . .'

The shock in his eyes made her break off. That sudden sharp look that came over his face told her that he was receiving her message, that he was dissecting it by adding the memory of the blush that had covered her when in the kitchen he had told her he was naked beneath his robe—this way the answer to his puzzlement at the 'Help me' plea he had seen in her eyes that time.

'Good God!' he muttered on a shattered breath. And as if still not believing her, 'You're not a . . .'

Defiantly, she cut him off, 'Yes, I am, and if you laugh at me, I'll . . .'

'Laugh at you!'

'Oh, shut up,' snapped Kelsey, and feeling a fool, did the only thing she knew to do to get him to shut up if he was going to laugh or, alternatively, get tough because she had lied to him. She leaned over and she kissed him.

To feel his mouth unresponsive beneath hers gave a nudge to the thoughts she had had that he had intended all along to reject her. But on pulling back from him, her face scarlet, she saw there were still traces of shock in him from what she had told him. But the fact that he wasn't roaring with laughter now he had the chance, made her stay and hope it wasn't rejection that had kept him from returning her kiss.

'There,' she said, swallowing down fresh nerves. 'You know now why I—haven't said anything about—er—wanting you before.'

She thought his mouth was starting to turn up at the corners, and hastily, expecting that now she would hear his bellow of laughter, she looked away. But the laugh she was expecting did not come. She waited another second, and then seeing no laughter there had the courage to go on.

'I discovered I was—sh-shy,' she brought out painfully. And when he still didn't appear to be amused, 'I know I shouldn't be after the way—the way . . .'

'The way we've made love before?' he suggested soberly, a softness there in his voice she welcomed, because suddenly he was sounding sensitive to her, sounding as if he—understood.

She nodded, but she still wasn't looking at him. 'I know it's ridiculous,' she said, 'but I can't help feeling a little—er . . .' she searched for a word, and brought out, 'nervous.'

'Not to say downright scared,' Serle put in quietly. And, his voice gentle, or so she thought, 'No wonder it's taken you so long to come to me!'

Relief started up in her at his quiet understanding. And when rejection no longer seemed to be likely, her nerves started to jump again as she started to confess, 'I just knew you would leave me—floundering, if I came and you didn't—didn't take me up on my . . .'

Her relief was shortlived. For on Serle coming in to offer the word she was seeking, Kelsey knew for sure that he *was* laughing at her—and in laughing at her, rejecting her after all—when teasingly, though she didn't see it as teasing, he suggested:

'Overtures?'

That put an end to it as far as she was concerned. With all manner of emotions rioting through her, she tried to scramble from the bed. The devil, he'd been stringing her along all this time! Why, the minute she slammed that door he'd be laughing his head off. And she'd thought to start a marriage! To save a marriage! Like hell she'd try to save it!

Why Serle was holding on to her so she couldn't get free of the tangle she was making of the covers over her, when he must only be waiting for her to be gone before he cracked his ribs laughing—unexpectedly polite of him, since he had never waited for her to be out of earshot to laugh before—Kelsey couldn't fathom. But hold on to her he did, and even had the audacity to ask:

'Where do you think you're going?'

'Back to my own bed!' she stormed, hitting at the hands that were holding her. And, panicking that she couldn't get free, 'Somehow or other this farce of a marriage is going to be annulled!'

'May I, as the mere husband, ask what grounds you

propose to use?' he enquired, quiet where she was violent.

Wildly she sought for an answer. 'Non-consummation!' she spat at him. But she was then having to fight the treachery in her as well as him, for he was taking his firm hold from her arms, and just as firmly he was placing his arms around her and drawing her close, his mouth close to her ear, as he murmured:

'Oh, I couldn't allow that.'

At the implication behind that remark Kelsey turned, frozen, stunned, to stare at him. Then the next thing she knew, Serle was taking advantage of her being speechless, for it was then that, gently, he laid his mouth over hers. Her heart beating like a wild thing within her, Kelsey suddenly lost her fight to be free. With Serle gently kissing her, she no longer wanted to fight.

The trembling that had started up in her could not be hidden. And she knew that Serle was aware of it when, taking his mouth from hers, only warmth in his eyes, softly he told her:

'I know that you're scared. And I know that your nerves are in uproar so that you hardly know what you're saying, but I want to stay married to you, little Kelsey.'

Having delivered his message that in his bed was where she was going to stay, he gently kissed her again. And it was gently that he moved her until she was lying with the pillow beneath her head, his hands coming to the sides of her face, soothing, as her heart pounding wildly, he made no attempt to take up his advantage gained on having quieted her.

'I'm not an ogre,' he continued softly, such warmth in him that she wanted to tell him that she wasn't afraid of him, more—nervous of uncharted waters, 'merely a man who wants you because . . .' He broke off, and was kissing her again, and Kelsey forgot, as his kiss gently deepened, that he had not told her why he wanted her.

But there was no doubt that soon she would have no grounds for that annulment.

'I'll take you as gently as I can, little love,' he said, pausing to kiss the two bright flares of colour that suddenly appeared on her cheeks. 'Don't be afraid of my touch where no other man's touch has strayed.'

She felt his hands gently caressing her, poetry in his movements as he eased the thin straps of her nightdress away and stroked her pulsating breasts. The thought of holding back never entering her head. Kelsey knew only that she wanted him. Even while she had to regret that he did not love her, Serle was stirring a passion in her, a gentle passion; for that was the way he was arousing her to want him. And that being so, when she felt his hand warm, tender against the naked skin of her hip, her small involuntary start beyond her control but stilling him, causing him to look steadily into her eyes, she could do no other than let him know that she had no objection to his hands being anywhere he cared to place them.

'I'm not afraid, Serle,' she said shakily, and at his slow smile that saluted her half lie, 'I want you,' she had to confess, the moment before he kissed her.

'There's no hurry,' he said quietly, his mouth leaving hers to plant tender kisses on her innocent eyes.

Kelsey smiled softly, and opened her eyes to see he was looking at her so tenderly that she just had to whisper, 'Oh, how I wish . . .' She choked back the rest of it, that she wished he would look at her as tenderly when they were not making love.

'What is it you wish, sweetheart?' he asked, making her want to deny that she wished for anything when he looked at her like that, as though anything in the world she desired he would get for her.

She rather suspected that in the heat of passion, however gentle, a man might promise anything. But this was something Serle could not get for her, because she wanted his love, and his love for her was something that just could not be conjured up because she wanted it.

But, 'What is it?' he was asking again, making her want that she had not said anything. 'Can you not tell me?' he pressed softly.

'You—said I was a romantic,' she excused, and did not think of lying as she saw he would not be satisfied until he knew what it was. 'I just wish,' she said, and swallowed as his hand stroked gently down the side of her face and had to look away from him, 'that – that you loved me a little.'

She thought, as that hand ceased caressing, that she had just killed the desire in him stone dead. And, wanting him so very badly, she could have cried that instead of accepting this time of tenderness with him, she had wanted more than he could give.

But then that hand was on the move again, and though she could feel the tension that had filled him, his hand had taken hold of her chin, and he was making her look at him.

'It's important to you,' he asked, his eyes searching her eyes, 'important that I—love you a little?'

Dearly did she want to deny it. But when she found the lie of 'No' that it was not important in any way at all, with Serle's sincere blue eyes seeking nothing but the truth, that lie refused to be uttered.

'Y-yes,' she whispered after a mighty struggle.

'Because you need love to be there—this first time of giving yourself?' he probed, that tension still taut in him.

Again Kelsey wanted to lie, this time wanting to agree, 'Yes'. But Serle seemed to be searching into her very soul, and she found, sadly, that she could not answer him at all, save to just look back at him, tears she despised herself for coming into her eyes. Tears which Serle, never taking his gaze from her, could not miss.

And suddenly that tension she had felt in him was

straining to breaking point. She could feel it, almost touch it as he went to look away from her glistening eyes, but she did not, because he seemed unable to. Then all at once that tension in him did snap, and she was left staring at him when, with a groan that sounded like a groan of defeat, he said hoarsely:

'Oh God, Kelsey, I can't hold out any longer—not when you look at me like that!' And while she had not an earthly idea of what was coming, he was cupping her face with both hands, and was telling her, 'Your wish is granted, my darling. There is more than a little love in me for you.' And as she stared transfixed, his eyes not leaving her, he told her tenderly, 'I love you to distraction, my dearest one.'

Thunder in her heart, a whole tropical storm going on inside of her, Kelsey looked back stupefied. 'You—love me?' she choked on a thread of breath, and for all of five seconds as without a smile, seriously he met her look, she was a mass of hope and sublime belief.

That was before she fell to earth with the most terrible, heart-wrenching thud. She had learned to trust Serle, but to have him lie to her, of all times now, scattered all the love in her. Not trying to comprehend how she could be so warm and loving to him only seconds ago, yet now, feeling betrayed that he could lie to her, thinking she would want such dishonesty, Kelsey was seized by such a sudden coldness of feeling towards him that it negated instantly everything that had gone before.

Her tears dried, the only tears were those inside her heart as she pushed at his chest over her. 'There was no need to lie to me!' she cried, her voice fracturing as, seeing she was panicking to be free, Serle allowed her to sit up. 'I don't want or need lies from you,' she told him chokily.

His arms firm about her prevented her from going anywhere. Or was it the hope in her heart that refused to know when it was beaten that stayed her when, sounding never more sincere, she heard over her shoulder:

'I wasn't lying.'

As frozen as she had suddenly become inside, Kelsey found that hope, that still unbelieving hope, made her turn in his arms so she could see into his face.

'Yes, you were,' she accused. But there was no strength in her accusation, because Serle was looking as sincere as he had sounded. Though she didn't miss the thread of steel that was there as he said clearly, his eyes not looking anywhere but into hers:

'I am in love with you, Kelsey Falconer—believe it.'

Wanting to cry, to laugh, to allow the joy in her to break forth, she knew that Serle telling her he loved her just had to be too unbelievable to be true. Though since she did not like at all that his gentle look for her had gone—perversely as the ice in her started to melt as suddenly as it had formed she wanted his gentle look back again, and she was less forthright than she had been when she questioned his declaration.

'It wasn't just—lovemaking talk?' she asked, her ridiculous heart playing havoc within her.

'I have never,' he replied, 'under *any* circumstances, told any woman that I loved her.'

Nerves had her fingers going to her chin, hope soaring to hear that no matter how much he had been involved before, she was the first female he had ever said those words to that meant so much

'You mean it?' she asked huskily, her hand coming away from her chin, that hand wanting to touch his bare shoulder, to plead with him to let it be true. There again, were tears in her eyes but not from sadness this time. 'You really mean it, Serle?' she begged, and pleaded without touching him, pride having no place any more, 'You really—love me?'

For long unspeaking seconds Serle looked back at her, and Kelsey felt tension in him again the longer he looked. Then, that harshness in him fading, slowly, he was saying:

'It sounds of some—consequence to you.' And with his eyes still searching in her, quietly he added, 'Of more consequence than I would have . . .' He broke off, then suddenly, tensely, he was gripping her naked arms, the pressure increasing as, not looking for lies either, he asked, 'Just *how* important is it to you, Kelsey, to know that I love you?'

For ageless moments she stared into those sharp blue eyes. Then with the sound of her heart roaring a crescendo in her ears, she saw the traces of a smile touch the corners of his mouth. And blindingly clearly then, she saw that Serle was not going to laugh his head off if she confessed just how important his love was to her, but that, with that gentleness she had discovered in him lurking round the corner, his smile was a smile of encouragement. And that could only mean, she thought, her heart threatening to burst, that he wanted to hear of her love, that he—wanted her love.

'Oh, Serle,' she cried, her hands going up to his shoulders, her joy knowing no bounds at the feel of him, 'I love you so much, and have done ever since . . .'

It was as far as she got. With a roar that was not a laugh, Serle hauled her against him. And though perhaps it was not very lover-like to be called a wretched woman as he told her she had put him through hell, to Kelsey, locked in his arms, it was the most romantic thing she had ever heard.

'I still can't believe it,' she breathed, not wondering how she now came to be lying down, Serle propped up on an elbow gazing down at her. For as he looked adoringly at her, forward or no, she could not refrain from telling him, 'I'm so glad I found the courage to come through that door tonight.'

'Had you not done so, my beloved Kelsey, I would have come and fetched you,' he confessed, owning when she stared at him in surprise, 'I was planning to give you only another two minutes, when the door was pushed open and there you were.' He smiled as he remembered. 'I didn't need any second invitation not to hog all of the bed to myself, did I?'

Kelsey blushed, and was kissed for her blushes, as she in turn confessed, 'I had to make myself angry before I could come through that door.'

'I now realise why, my love,' he told her tenderly. 'Try not to think of me as such a swine for wanting you to make the first move. But I've never been in love before, and it knocked me all of a heap,' he explained. 'I've suffered agonies of jealousy thinking of you with other men, yet even married to me you didn't think enough of me to come to me.—Yet you had to come to me because you wanted to.'

'Oh, darling,' she whispered, his pain her pain, 'I didn't know.' Then she smiled as she saw he need have no reason to be jealous now, had had no reason to be jealous then. 'I'll never lie to you again,' she promised.

When that promise had been sealed with a kiss, content for the moment just to be able to look at him with open love showing in her eyes, it occurred to Kelsey that Serle hadn't been all that open with her either.

'You've been a little—er—not so straightforward yourself, as I recall,' she murmured, loving the way his fingers were tracing backwards and forwards over her shoulder.

'More than a little,' he admitted with a wry grin. 'To start with there was this pert, beautiful English girl who stormed in from nowhere one day and tore me of a strip over something which I had no knowledge of.'

Kelsey tried to look shamefaced as she recalled that day she had gone marching into his office, but with a smile on her mouth the shamefaced look didn't quite come off.

'Then,' he teased, 'the next thing I know, the same pert female is trying to make me look about two inches high in front of some V.I.P.s whom the firm need to have confidence in us.'

'You looked murderous,' Kelsey murmured, her smile gone. 'Will you forgive me?'

'I'll forgive you anything providing you'll always love me,' said Serle tenderly.

He kissed her again then, a long lingering kiss, that left her breathless, and tingling, and wanting more. And when he took his mouth away from hers she could see from the fire that was in his eyes that it was the same for him too.

Though when instead of taking up the invitation in her eyes he pulled back to again prop himself up on his elbow and looked at her, she was remembering his, 'There's no hurry,' from before. She saw then that there was still a lot to be said between them, old ghosts to be dealt with, and that while his eyes were telling her that he was as eager for her as she was for him, Serle was not a grab fast type of man, her heart beat erratically as she suddenly realised that Serle wanted to set a gradual, easy pace for this first time for her.

'You were—er—saying,' she reminded him, trying desperately hard to remember what it was they had been talking about, as she tried equally hard to control the yearning he had again triggered off in her.

'Was I?' he murmured teasingly, letting her know her attempt to keep cool was not fooling him for a moment.

'About—about that time—er—Yukiko and I saw you in that restaurant,' she recalled, giving herself full marks.

'So I was,' he grinned. 'Well, luckily I was able to complete the business with my luncheon guests satisfactorily. But, not to put too fine a point on it, I really thought then that it was about time you learned a few manners.'

Having asked his forgiveness once for her appalling behaviour, about to do so again, she remembered the way he had set about teaching her a few manners, by sending the polite go-between to see her father.

'You remembered what I'd said about an arranged marriage definitely not being for me?' she asked instead.

'It was all too perfect,' Serle recalled. 'I knew you'd be as mad as hell, but,' he confessed, 'I was as mad as hell too.' Suddenly a grin he couldn't control was breaking from him as he recalled, 'And did I have proof that you were mad! "The daughter of Marchant-*san* is willing," Mr Saito told me, and then he handed me the picture you'd sent.'

'I—er—was a little cross,' said Kelsey demurely.

'A non-starter in understatement,' Serle smiled. 'You might have passed the verbal message back, "I'm willing", but there was no mistaking the more truthful "Get lost, Falconer" look in your eyes. Forgive me, my love, but who could resist the challenge in your flashing eyes, who could resist trying to string you along?'

'Not you,' she answered happily, when no answer was necessary. 'So having received my reply, you took up the gauntlet, and arranged that restaurant meeting with my father and me.'

'And what a meeting! I didn't know how I managed to keep my face straight, with you trying to keep it from showing that you wouldn't mind going in for knife throwing.'

'I thought I did rather well,' Kelsey commented, and remembered, 'You kissed me that night and . . .'

'And began falling in love with you,' he said softly.

'Then?' she exclaimed, thinking of all that had gone on, all the time that had elapsed and she hadn't known!

'I felt some strange something happening to me when I had you no longer fearful of what I was going to do to you. I looked at you and found that I couldn't breathe. I think I was in some shock myself,' he admitted. 'And *then* I kissed you, and your response was something else again, and I knew that this thing called love I'd heard about but had never before experienced—didn't fully believe in,' he owned, 'was on the lookout for another scalp.'

Wide-eyed, Kelsey still could not credit that he had known so long. 'You knew then!' was all she was capable of gasping.

'I told myself I was wrong,' he replied, 'and spent all the following Sunday trying to get you out of my mind.'

'Oh,' she said softly, her brain waking up as she came away from the startling surprise he had given her. 'Is that why, when you come calling the next day, you came with roses in your hand?'

'Sorry, my darling,' Serle confessed gently, 'it wasn't quite like that. The roses were meant, but as a cover.'

'Cover?'

'I was knocked all of a heap, like I said. In all my adult life I've never been so unsure of myself. I needed to cover this new thing that had happened to me. The roses were a last-minute idea—I knew you wouldn't take me seriously if I came calling with roses in my hand—that you would think I was just hamming it up for all I was worth. I've been covering up ever since,' he ended.

'Oh, Serle,' she murmured. 'To think you've known you love me since then, and that I've known I was in love with you since that night you rang and said you thought we should have a serious talk, and yet we've . . .'

'You've known since then?' It was Serle's turn to be incredulous. Then he was kissing her gently, then drawing back, he too mourning the time they had wasted as he went on to tell her of moments when he had thought she had seen through his cover. Revealing that the day he had stood with her at the Tededori dam, when she had looked so adorable and trusting that he had wanted to kiss her and ask her to marry him, but having been trying to gain her confidence, he had seen almost too late that the time wasn't right. Telling her how when she had told him she wasn't going to see him again he'd had to think fast, he tried to find out if she felt anything at all for him when he'd asked her if it was more than a game to her, and getting that same response from her when again he had kissed her, he had thought of sending the money hoping she would give it to her father and not send it back.

'You meant my father to have it all along?'

'It was a small price to pay if I could keep you in Japan.' And while she was faintly staggered that he could dismiss the twenty thousand so lightly, he was saying, 'I needed a hold on you, Kelsey my darling. You were just as likely to take it into your head to leave Japan as stay—I wanted you to stay.'

'Oh, Serle,' she whispered, 'and I never knew! All that time you were covering . . .'

'And nearly had my cover blown the night I called to ask your father if he had any objection to my marrying you,' he broke in to tell her, which made her remember:

'You asked me then if I'd heard more than my father asking if you'd called to ask for my hand.'

'And I was sweating like a schoolboy on your answer,' he said, to her amazement.

'You were?'

'I guess I've been as scared of you finding out I loved you as you were scared I would find out how you felt about me,' he owned—then told her, 'Had you been in earshot before then, you would have heard me telling him that my love for you was too personal, went too deep, for me to want a stranger to act on my behalf any longer.'

'Oh, darling!' Kelsey cried, and whether Serle wanted to pace their lovemaking slowly or not, she could no longer stop from stretching up her arms to him.

Serle must have decided that any other explanations could wait, for he needed no second bidding to gather her up close and hold her as though he never intended to let her go.

It was broad daylight when Kelsey awakened, the day already well on its way. But even not fully awake yet, she seemed to know that the lateness of the hour didn't matter—that today was something different.

Serle! As Serle jumped into her mind, she was fully awake. She turned on her side, her heart pounding with fear that she had imagined all that had happened.

'Good morning, my own sweet love,' said the man propped up on an elbow beside her, watching her as he had last night.

'Hello,' she said huskily, searing hot colour covering every part of her, knowledge there that though she was his wife now, she still felt a shyness that could make her crimson when she thought of the way they had been.

'I thought you'd never wake,' Serle said softly, a hand coming out to gently brush a tousled strand of fair hair back from her face, that same hand stroking understandingly down the blush of her cheek.

'H-have you been—awake long?' she stammered.

'Not nearly long enough to have my fill of your beauty,' he murmured.

'Oh, Serle,' Kelsey cried, 'I love you so—yet . . .'

She didn't get to finish, for suddenly she was in his arms, against his heart. 'It's all right, my darling,' he shushed her. 'Don't . . .'

'It's not all right,' she wailed, scalding tears falling down her face. And urgently, so he must know how much she loved him, 'I'd thought several times that you might reject me—I just—just hadn't given a thought—th-that I might try to reject you.'

'It was the pain I caused you my darling, not you,' he soothed, cradling her, so understanding of her; of those moments of searing pain that had seen her trying to push him away, her cries of 'No' stifled by his mouth gentle on hers, by tenderly murmured endearments until the pain had gone and she had choked, 'Oh, darling, I'm sorry,' and had moved to him, only to cry out again and try again to reject him as she felt new pain.

'I love you so much, Serle,' she said, her face coming out of hiding as she lifted it up for his kiss.

'I know you do,' he assured her tenderly. 'Just as you know I love you.'

Kelsey nodded, and felt his fingers, tender still, smooth away her tears. Then gently he was kissing her, his kiss becoming more urgent as she pressed her naked form against him, wanting to get nearer to him, not starting with shyness this morning as his hands on her bare hips pressed her still closer to him.

An ache was being fired in her to feel him yet closer, and feverishly now her hands roved him as if she would make up for the dreadful time it must have been for him last night.

The feel of his strong muscular back beneath her hands had her crying softly, 'I won't reject you ever again,' that ache in her to feel him with her once more.

Gently Serle moved her until her back was against the mattress, his mouth pressing her as he came to lie half over her. She saw the flush of desire on his face, and her panicky feelings that she had driven him from wanting her by the way she had been before were quieted when softly, his voice husky, he breathed:

'Oh God, Kelsey, you're so wonderful, I never knew such joy could be mine!'

And joy was hers too, when treating her as gently as he had before, kissing her, tenderly caressing her, Serle at last came to her again. But this time there was no pain to stop her need to give him her all—and as passion mounted, stretched higher and ever higher towards that topmost peak, Serle was wringing from her a passion such as she had never had a hint that she possessed.

'Oh, how I love you, my beloved wife,' he said, when later they lay with her head on his shoulder, her breast beneath his hand. 'You're just too . . .' there wasn't a word that would fit, 'marvellous,' he short-listed.

Kelsey, basking in the wonder of his lovemaking, in the wonder of him, in the wonder that he loved her, stirred beside him and turned her head up to look at him.

The love she saw there for her in his face made her

swallow, and careless of time, she asked, 'Do you have to go to work today?'

Serle moved her to her side, the front of her body facing him, wanting her that close for the pure togetherness of it, then she saw him grin broadly.

'What—work on my honeymoon?' he teased.

Kelsey smiled, her right arm going over his shoulder, the tips of her breasts pressing against him. 'I'm glad Mrs Kaido doesn't come to clean today,' she gurgled. She was positively chuckling, her breasts moving against his chest, when, nibbling her ear, Serle broke off to say in a low growl:

'I'll send word to tell her not to come tomorrow either.'